Penguin Books

Kenzo: a Tokyo story

Ross Davy was born in Brisbane, and has lived in
Melbourne and Tokyo. *Kenzo: a Tokyo story* is his
first novel. His work has appeared in journals such as
Meanjin and *Mattoid* and in Japanese translation by
Professor Michio Ochi for a volume of Australian
stories. He has studied various things, among them,
art, and is working on a second novel.

Leginread me, release!

www.Bookcrossing.com
BCID 796-6613397

Ross Davy

Kenzo: a Tokyo story

Penguin Books

Publication assisted by
the Literature Board of the Australia Council,
the Federal Government's arts funding and advisory body

Penguin Books Australia Ltd,
487 Maroondah Highway, P.O. Box 257
Ringwood, Victoria, 3134, Australia
Penguin Books Ltd,
Harmondsworth, Middlesex, England
Penguin Books,
40 West 23rd Street, New York, N.Y. 10010, U.S.A.
Penguin Books Canada Ltd,
2801 John Street, Markham, Ontario, Canada
Penguin Books (N.Z.) Ltd,
182-190 Wairau Road, Auckland 10, New Zealand

First published by Penguin Books Australia, 1985
Reprinted 1985

Copyright © Ross Davy, 1985

Typeset in 90% Bodoni Book by Leader Composition Pty Ltd, Melbourne

Made and printed in Australia
by The Dominion Press-Hedges & Bell

CIP

Davy, Ross. 1953-

Kenzo: a Tokyo story

ISBN 0 14 007707 3.

1. Title

A823'.3

Acknowledgements and thanks go to among others Bruce Sims for editing and production; Helen Semmler for the cover illustration; Kim Roberts for design; and to Jackie Yowell especially.

A short section of the novel first appeared in *Mattoid* magazine in a slightly different form.

The characters and incidents in this novel are fictional and have no relation to persons or events, living or dead.

The character 'Linda' is not intended as a demonstration of ideas about women in relation to spirit.

To Hasna and Moko,
two great lady friends

Part
One

Kenzo runs across the busy street and mounts the steps of the pedestrian bridge which crosses over the busiest intersection in Shibuya. The red sun hangs engorged in the grey-mauve evening sky. The smog makes the sun seem even fuller and larger than it really should be at that position in the sky. The neons prick and trickle in the August sky. Like immense liners at berth the blazing sides of the department stores shore up to the right, and to the left rise the high freeways where tons of roaring metal move west.

It is the first week of the summer holidays and Kenzo's third-year exams at the Daikuma Buddhist university have finished. He feels light and free after marinading in the Pali scriptures for all those months. The beginning of the next semester is in September. Zen priestdom, in his father's temple, waits in the distance.

He dismisses the thought. For tonight, at least, he can do as he pleases, have a Saturday night, get drunk maybe.

Having crossed the footbridge he can see Tatsuo his lover waiting slouched on one hip outside a department store. The crowd with its distracting density is stage scenery which prevents Tatsuo from seeing Kenzo too soon, before Kenzo enters the light Tatsuo is the cause and centre of.

Tatsuo is the same age as Kenzo and is also a student – a research student studying computers and computer music at the Tokyo College of Music. He has access to tape decks, pianos, scored sheets and technicians skilled in showing him the ways of the mysterious and fabulous computer. He is showing progress in the application of his music to computers. Kenzo has heard the tape of Tatsuo's first composition. It is good. Kenzo envies him.

In front of the department store Tatsuo is handsome in jeans and a t-shirt with the sleeves rolled up over his smooth brown shoulders. His short black hair is sleek on his neck marked by two small moles. Kenzo can make them out from here. He can also sees how Tatsuo's nipples make tiny points under his t-shirt. Now Kenzo is coming close enough to be able to make out the line of Tatsuo's penis under the denim. Kenzo likes Tatsuo's long foreskin, as easy as a suede glove finger one minute then tight as pulled silk the next. Any second now every angle of Tatsuo's body will realign with rapid grace on recognition of Kenzo.

The edge of the crowd moves apart like difficult but obedient scenery. Tatsuo sees Kenzo. Kenzo rushes up to him. They push each other for boyish joy.

And wait for their Australian friend Linda who is always late. An English teacher as well as being a student of Buddhism and many other miscellaneous things besides, she is late from probably having stopped to chat to a yakitori-seller or maybe from having had to turn back to punch someone on the train who had put his hand up her dress. Her train journeys are never dull. Nor is she who is the epitome of joy and zest for life. Shortly, swinging grins and a shoulder bag, Linda lobs herself into the crowd like a bomb. People push aside. Tatsuo and Kenzo give her a friendly shove each and they all laugh.

(A few minutes ago, when Kenzo was just about to cross the footbridge, something started to go haywire in his brain. A tension was now starting to expand as gas heated in a bottle.

Kenzo had no ostensible awareness he'd just become a thing which would not be able to contain its destruction. A hit and run victim on the intersection of time and matter.)

Into a black box disco hurtling neon-lacquered through the night they enter. Cartwheeling light and colour. It is Kenzo's first time here. Tatsuo leads Kenzo and Linda in. Tatsuo seems to, with his cheeky diagonal of a smile, know everyone here. He is already dancing on the spot while having the change for his drink counted into his hand. Linda also is in her element though it's a gay disco. She is laughing and smiling and the people are swirling around her. It is all so fascinating to Kenzo. He wonders impudently if his father, in his evening meditation, has come across a vision of where his son is now. But what does it matter? Tatsuo is luring them onto the dance floor and Kenzo is now dancing though he thought he didn't know how to. Whiskies and beers make them steadily drunker and merrier. Except Tatsuo. He is glancing at his watch. It is ten-thirty. He has to be up early tomorrow morning to go to Okinawa for a holiday. He hasn't told Kenzo when he intends to return. He leaves. Abrupt and secret and smiling.

Kenzo might stop to wonder for a moment.

But no sooner have Kenzo and Linda danced five more minutes than two boys dance closer – one – a long drink of water, in black, with a Nefertiti-head perched forward on an elegant stalk of a neck. He suddenly bites Kenzo's hair and puts his tongue in his ear. Kenzo doesn't know what to do. Linda and the boy's friend laugh at them. That boy – Yoshiki – the friend informs Linda, has had Kenzo marked out all night. Kenzo follows Yoshiki back to the bar counter, pinches him and asks for a light for his cigarette. Kenzo has smoked too much already but he doesn't know how to stop so nervous is he with Yoshiki now curling around him like a snake.

By eleven Linda has vanished leaving Kenzo to accept the consequences of her high spirits. Yoshiki is giving Kenzo impatient and langourous stares. Kenzo suddenly feels he couldn't give a damn about anything. Because he can do everything and doesn't have to do anything. They head for a 'Love Hotel' nearby and pad their way drunkenly up the musty carpeted stairs with a key-jangling crone bringing up the rear. They are locked into a room? No. Kenzo discovers he can leave to take a shower. Down the hall he sways like a ship under the storm of drunkenness.

When he returns Yoshiki is lolling on the bed rubbing away an imaginary headache with two fingers on his temples. Then it is inevitable that they go through the motions of making love. Yoshiki's skin is as smooth and dry as a snake's. Kenzo perspires and is convinced his genitals stink as Yoshiki stuffs them into his mouth. Soon enough it becomes clear that Kenzo will never achieve an erection with Yoshiki. The orchestra stops. Someone stands up and asks Why? Why? Kenzo doesn't know why. Yoshiki tries to liquidate him with his melting eyes. Too much sugar and gelatine in those looks for Kenzo's liking. To defend his dignity Kenzo has to make up a story and tell Yoshiki he can't get aroused because he can't stop thinking guiltily of his last lover who died a month ago of liver cancer. Thirty-six, wife and two children. It was tragic. Kenzo goes quiet. Yoshiki is convinced. Leaves Kenzo alone.

They try to sleep. Kenzo lies awake in disbelief at this night. This is the first time he's ever lain with anyone other than Tatsuo. Why is | 5 he doing it? – Drunk, he surmises. He used to be so faithful to Tatsuo that what he's doing now bewilders him.

In the middle of the night the air-conditioning fails and the room becomes as stuffy and lethal as a Black Hole of Calcutta. As well, Kenzo's pillow increases in height so as to crick his neck. Also he develops a sore throat and has to reach across the slumbering Yoshiki for his cold capsules. So he doesn't sleep. Is kept awake with horror and amazement at the tale he spun to poor Yoshiki.

In the morning, on waking, Yoshiki flutters and lights a cigarette and asks Kenzo if he wants tea. Of course he wants tea. Anything. Yoshiki swirls up winding the sheet Paris gown-fashion around his nakedness and trips over to the window, opens it, peeks outside, then empties the tiny teapot out of it. Kenzo bites the pillow so as not to laugh.

They drink tea. Yoshiki puts his head on an inquisitive angle and croons. They smoke. Get dressed. Leave. Pass the old lady at the door whom Kenzo could swear made a move to pat him on the backside.

Kenzo disposes of Yoshiki as soon as possible after two cups of coffee, two salads, two pizzas, and after giving him his fan as a souvenir. Yoshiki flits off down the street fanning himself, in the sunlight a damaged butterfly.

Kenzo brushes the powder off his fingers.

Kenzo feels drunkenly wonderful riding the train home which is going as fast as a jet. The windows are open and the blinds beat in the wind. Feeling nothing in particular now Kenzo walks the cool green streets back to where he boards. A convex traffic mirror shoots his reflection into the sky as he turns the corner opposite. He walks past an old farmhouse which up until now hasn't caught his attention. But today, this early Sunday afternoon, it arouses his curiosity. A tall metal frame structure is standing in the yard. It is partially covered by canvas. A trapeze wire is stretched from one pole to another above a trampoline. A girl in jeans wearing a bathing cap is gingerly stepping out on the wire. She is not going to fall. Her friends are below with pursed mouths. One of them throws up an opened parasol to the girl and she deftly catches it. Kenzo admires her. He looks around. There are huge pieces of half-painted scenery leaning against the trees. There is a merry-go-round horse rearing forever in a clump of silent wild flowers. Clapping draws his attention back.

The girl has crossed the wire in triumph. She is now attempting to go back again. Who are these people? Kenzo must find out. He picks his way over wire, rock and paint pot to address himself to the group. They turn. They smile. They are dressed in coloured singlets and are sunburnt on the backs of their necks. Kenzo likes them. He asks them what they are doing and they answer him – They are members of an underground theatre group based in Shinjuku but who practise their livelier acts in this farmyard. They are going to put on a play next Saturday they say. Will Kenzo come? Of course. They all squat down in the grass and someone brings out iced tea. They sit talking until dusk.

At eight this Sunday evening Kenzo got a phone call from Nicky – one of Linda's friends. Kenzo doesn't know whether he likes him or not. But Nicky wanted Kenzo to have dinner with him and a friend tomorrow night. It is important, Nicky said. Kenzo agreed to go. Nicky then told Kenzo why it was important. It took about an hour spliced in with anecdotes about how much money Nicky was spending lately and about how he'd left a contact lens in his shirt pocket and got it crushed at the dry cleaners.

Kenzo then put the phone down and looked through some of his dreary notes on Theravada Buddhism only to close them up again almost immediately.

He is now lying on his bed trying not to think of anything, least of all of Tatsuo. Suddenly he hits the wall in a rage. And then starts laughing, just as suddenly.

The early morning sun falls brightly through the window, down along the stuffy air behind the locked glass windows to make the one united shadow of the anywhere positions of the piano, flute and kettle drum in the small room. It is very quiet. A bike passes under the windows. A roof beam creaks. A board in the pier creaks under the momentary pressure of someone diving into the warm tropical water. The aqua and turquoise water shakes and closes over his head. The sun falls onto the sea. A sound in the air. People laugh on the beach.

Ten minutes late. Monday night. Kenzo's mood was rotten. Askew in the head.

What made me agree to come here?

Nicky and Jiro appeared to have been waiting crouched behind the ticket machines. The way they sprang out. The width of Nicky's crocodile smile encompassing the first horrible seconds of the meeting. Nicky's relief that Kenzo had shown up at all. The rings of Nicky's fingers, the bells on his toes now. His exaggerated Michelangeloesque beard and profile. The leering face. Mr Smooth. A lizard tongue keeping his lips permanently wet and red. Behind the smile, metal faeces and mildew. Strong after-shave lotion. Always the window-shopper. An ugliness in him coming off on you like grease. His clear-cut vulgarity makes you feel in his presence like either a prim old pressed violet or a fellow pirate. In his better moments he does seem like a pirate, hairy bare-chested on the rigging of a situation, laughing jeeringly at whoever and whatever. However, no pirate bitches as much as Nicky does as to whether his jacket is getting crushed or his pants wet in the rain. Dislikable, he is by no means unlovable though. Easy enough for Japanese to fall for the Mr America toothpaste smile and profile. Poor pigeon-shit Jiro was such a victim – and now, unwanted prey.

Kenzo faced Jiro – short, jeans, hairdo too stylish for his miserable face. Minimised introductions. Outside – typhoonal rain. They all ran as if being chased or chasing up the booming swaying street hellish with red lanterns and Nicky's cracked shrieks.

They fell into the restaurant soaked with rain and sweat, all possible moods nipped in the bud as they squatted on the cushions pretending to be getting comfortable. The neighbours leaning towards them. Ears opening to catch anything they might say. All leaned back when Nicky began protesting about the high prices on the menu even though Jiro was paying. Paying dearly for vows taken while masturbating. The beer, the sashimi and the other courses arrived and passed woodenly under their eyes, everything almost as tasteless as they. Yes, tasteless and sad.

For according to Nicky, in Sunday night's phone conversation a week before, Jiro had made his first excursion into a gay bar which was also the night of Nicky's 101st. What was Jiro after as he sat in the smoky corner biting the rim of his gin glass? Nothing probably, thinking about his first and only lover of two years previous when he was twenty-four. And since then nothing but hate for gay bars and

8 |

promiscuity and furtive monthly masturbations into neatly folded wads of tissue paper with the famous vow on his lips to love only one person into the grave if he ever found that person.

Jiro was recommended to that person by the fatefully friendly and over-doing-his-job bartender just as Nicky was about to leave. So Nicky led the pet out on a chain – routine business but surprising when Jiro asked to have a cup of coffee first before mounting the scaffold. There in the coffee shop Jiro told enough accidentally of his innocent self to stimulate the rather jaded Nicky but not quite enough to frighten him off. Nicky was soon envisaging a near future of discount hairstylings in one of Jiro's salons and maybe even a free bottle or two of conditioner. The rest of Jiro's short and pathetic story came out in Nicky's bed. Then, at first impotent, then wild as a puma from self-rage, Jiro well satisfied the connoisseur Nicky but the shortly following declarations and avowals of eternal love didn't. Nicky needs eternal love as much as a jackal needs knives and forks. Fortunately for Nicky, at eight am the next morning Jiro had to leave for work.

But during the day Nicky received four desperate phone calls from Jiro. Nicky's replies were direct and honest – No, he wasn't going to give up his promiscuous ways and settle for just Jiro. Nicky was a true lover of freedom. And besides, the beauty salons were on the other side of town, too far away anyway.

During the fourth phone call that evening, between his sobs, Jiro managed to cajole Nicky into meeting him for dinner the following Monday night. Nicky was persuadable only because he had begun thinking of Kenzo – the novice Zen priest, the fire-escape.

So now, Jiro was tearing his second napkin to shreds under the table as he began whispering hypnotically to Nicky: You're a Bad Man You're a Bad Man. Eyes fixed on Nicky, Jiro wasn't the slightest bit interested in Kenzo except when he wanted Kenzo to translate something difficult into English for Nicky. Nicky's plan for getting Jiro and Kenzo together looked like falling through. It was hard to tell who was being the most ridiculous. Kenzo only wished he could have been watching the whole thing on television at home. None of them wanted to be there.

After Jiro threw a pair of chopsticks at the laughing Nicky all they could do was leave. Their neighbours' ears shrank back into their heads.

Jiro pushed Kenzo and Nicky into a cab. They arrived at Jiro's favourite club – the 'Fontain Bleau', Jiro probably hoping a bit of luxury would soften Nicky up. The booth was so soft and dark Kenzo felt as if he were sitting inside a chocolate. Chandeliers swung on the hostesses' ears as they rested on the furniture like horseflies. One came over and settled on a footstool by Kenzo's knee. The effect of her black kimono was intentionally daunting. An oily pianist played some oily music.

The trio played with their drinks and snacks and Jiro seemed to be calming down. He threw no more chopsticks but was still as unpredictable as a teething child. When the hostess finally left them alone Jiro's face lit up and he told Nicky he didn't love him anymore. Let's only be friends. Nobody looked convinced but Jiro insisted on half standing up and shaking Nicky's hand. With that accomplished he strode over to the piano, took up the mike and sang a love song. Then Nicky was asked to sing too. He didn't need much persuasion. As the crocodile grin and the pointed beard multiplied in the wall mirrors, beside Kenzo Jiro sighed and looked ominously relaxed. What was he still expecting? Kenzo looked down at Jiro's knee and felt a perverse urge to pat it in sympathy.

In the cab going back to the station Jiro suddenly came out of his pleasant daze and nervously started twisting and squirming in his seat at the prospect of going home alone. He was really depressed. He wanted them all to have coffee together to prolong the evening . . . Then, Nicky turned and smugly said to Kenzo, 'I have to be going now, but you stay and have coffee with him. It's the least you can do after the lovely dinner he gave you.'

Linda is lying down on her bed staring at the opposite wall. She's not sick, just a bit sleepy and depressed. Staring at the wall reminds her of how one day just after her tenth birthday, when she was in bed with a heavy cold, she lay quietly looking around her room with the horse-riding competition pennants stuck up on the walls with the swimming certificates. In that dim and still and tediously unchanging room they were the only cheering things, along with the small circular mirror above the bookcase opposite her someone had thoughtfully put there to let her see the sky because the bed couldn't be moved to face the windows.

The clouds were occasionally moving across the sky in the mirror.

Linda now distinctly remembers how she was quietly taken with the beauty of that piece of sky, representing as it did the world outside and not being sick. She felt lonely then as she does now, wishing she could be out somewhere, living it up.

Then the funny thought comes to her now, that day, while staring at the sky in the mirror, she suddenly felt a powerful urge to become good and pure. Then Linda, becoming sleepier now, is not so sure if she really felt that urge then or just now, while thinking about it. She stares at the blank opposite wall and wishes there could be a mirror there now anyway, even though it's night.

Jiro opened the door to his apartment. Feeling foolish, cynical, cunning, depolarised, anxious and excited, propelled maybe by the unconsummated Saturday night before, Kenzo tiptoed in in his socks. Through the tiny kitchen he walked neither too quickly nor too slowly into the main room. He entered it calmly, trimming the corners off what his senses were taking in, correcting himself, trying to prove he still had some control.

Forgetting Kenzo was there, back turned, Jiro threw down the door keys with an arrogance that couldn't have been anything else but a slip of his more normal self. Kenzo smiled. Having put off recognition of Kenzo's presence till the last possible moment, Jiro turned, ran a hand through his still too upswept hair and gestured tragically around at the furniture for Kenzo's appraisal.

Very department store cabinets. Hemingway with whisky bottles inside instead of pages. Canadian autumn prints. Plastic grapes on the sideboard and a little personal computer for anonymous numerical daydreams. Too many things for one person. A haze of tawny port and furniture polish. Kenzo smiled a benevolent, noncommittal, lunatic's smile around the room as he sat back in the rocking-chair. The walls and ceiling itched to close in. Jiro poured – or rather, shook out brandy or something. Must have been brandy as there was only a little of it in the bottom of a balloon-glass. Jiro knocked his glass off the sideboard while trying to get down one of his hairdressing medals. Had to then bustle with the vacuum cleaner. A good opportunity then for Kenzo to examine everything more carefully. Wringing out the glass-powdered cloth in the kitchen Kenzo was touched by the neat, almost little girl's tea-party way Jiro had arranged the drying dishes under a cloth. Then, more objects stretched for attention – toothbrush, shampoo and razor on the shelf so subservient and pathetic in their quietness they seemed almost on the point of weeping for themselves. What a lonely person Jiro was. Almost no friends save clients and his staff. How lonely Kenzo himself now felt.

Back in the livingroom Kenzo and Jiro sat back and talked. At first Jiro's face was locked up but gradually Kenzo's careless yet pointedly interested questions caught him off guard. Jiro's face cautiously opened only to slam shut again. Kenzo was getting carried away with evoking any response out of Jiro he wanted. Finally, as if to shut Kenzo up Jiro came over to examine Kenzo's hairstyle in his official capacity as a hairdresser. Kenzo's hair grew straight up in front, then flopped forward to one side. Jiro's expert fingers, that much Kenzo enjoyed. But Jiro soon lost interest in Kenzo's hair. Priests shouldn't have hair anyway. He walked around the room. Trying to crack his knuckles. His anxiety was faintly electrical in Kenzo. What was Jiro going to do next? Spring at Kenzo like a wild cat or come up shyly like a dog to lick his hand? Kenzo had a moment then of deadening exhaustion of not knowing how to react to anything at all. He envied himself the possibility he could have been home now, contentedly smoking and picking his toenails while the last bars of some piece of music lingered in his ears.

Jiro saved him from any more confusion by announcing it was time for bed. To buy time Kenzo asked for something to sleep in. Out came an extraordinary, thick, very black and velvety shaving coat. With ridiculous modesty Kenzo changed into it in the kitchen while seeking reassuring tenderness from the sight of the prettily stacked dishes. Jiro absent-mindedly walked in and out in just his Dynamite-briefs as if the sight of his near nakedness couldn't possibly have stimulated Kenzo.

They lay down on the bedding as innocently as two teddy-bears. They listened to their watches tick. Kenzo asked Jiro to put his alarm clock in the drawer as it ticked too loudly. After he had done that while he was still up he got some more brandy, nuts and cigarettes. The way he set them out beside the futons was as intimate as the tea-party things in the kitchen but Kenzo was unmoved by it now. Seeing the objects actually being arranged destroyed their independence and pathos. Nevertheless Kenzo ate the nuts ravenously. Jiro finished off his brandy in a few gulps. Kenzo touched him on the cheek and they lightly kissed. It seemed alright. They frowned in concentration as if eating fish notorious for its bones. Once their teeth had found no obstacle, Kenzo was astonished at the ease of what they were doing.

It didn't last long. Jiro began flicking Kenzo's nipple with a steady viciousness. Bit him on the collar-bone. Kenzo likes rough stuff too sometimes so he bit him back. Then they had fun, enjoyed it almost as if they'd chosen each other.

But just as the semen was being brought to the boil, Jiro ruined everything by whimpering: 'The sheets, the sheets, they'll get messed!' But too late. His face twisted. He shot off. Then wrenched away, still jerking stumbling around the room blinded and then fell to his knees to pull handfuls of tissues out of a box to stuff into his groin. When Kenzo's bewildered hand touched Jiro's shoulder (he couldn't think of anything else to do as the last bars of the music in his private room rammed into his ears), Jiro pulled away and threw himself through the door onto the kitchen floor where he wept as dumbly as some primate injured by something it couldn't understand or see. The sight of a pale naked human being weeping on his knees on his own kitchen floor is not pleasant. Kenzo crept forward saying things, comforting things he thought. He thought he put his arms around Jiro and tried to be nice but that he can't be certain of.

Something trapped in the body, looking for air-vents and holes. Kenzo's eyes with Tatsuo in them couldn't shut. Couldn't stop peeking over at Jiro who had the cheek to lie as silently asleep as an effigy on a tomb. Kenzo envies the Japanese talent for sleeping in the face of no matter what crisis. Adorable peaceful little sub-consciousnesses, as tranquil as mud at the bottom of a lake. As for Kenzo, tossing and turning (admittedly, acting a little) among others, Freud and Jung and a Bodhisattva crossed their legs, began burning their midnight oil and set him a dreamless oral examination the questions of which were as idiotic and as unanswerable as was the hum of the air-conditioner in the kitchen or the dim buzz of the distant traffic.

Drowning men clutch at straws so Kenzo started forcing himself to somehow, somehow understand Jiro's behaviour, (rather than his own) – Jiro's anger and disappointment with Nicky, the breaking of his vows by letting himself allow Kenzo to let him succumb to Kenzo. But Freud and Jung were also shocked by how Kenzo's full erection frightened all sympathy away. His body, being its first priority, was standing out in front demanding to be sympathised with first. Pretending to be having a violent nightmare he could only kick the sleeping Jiro. Of course, Jiro didn't wake up.

About dawn Kenzo woke up. Must have been dawn as sounds were slowly on the increase outside. The space between the curtains showed a light blank sky where the tracks of the slow snail stars were fading. . . Morning was answering night but nothing was answering Kenzo's discomfort. Nothing could be done except go back to sleep again.

In the true morning Kenzo and Jiro unfortunately woke facing each other. Through a slit Kenzo had been watching Jiro's old child's face, the snub nose, the potential but undeveloped oracular promise of his brow and the large white teeth showing through his relaxed lips. On opening his eyes and seeing Kenzo watching him, Jiro's momentarily bright stare became shy and sunken and he put his arm over his face, turned away and groaned softly. He knew he was under an unspoken obligation. Kenzo smiled.

Soon enough Jiro shifted near Kenzo. The teeth and tongue went over Kenzo's erection which was so crackably hard it hurt. Kenzo came almost instantaneously, as if merely earthing a current. Jiro stumbled up glancing scornfully at Kenzo, ran his mouth full of semen into the kitchen, spat it down the sink and then vigorously brushed his teeth with as much toothpaste as he could squeeze.

They lay listening to Ravel on the stereo radio. Jiro became wooed and relaxed by the music, though undoubtedly thinking about Nicky. Sensing that and also now fully grasping the lovelessness with which Jiro had brought him off Kenzo decided to take advantage of him and rearouse him. Jiro liked Kenzo's brushstrokes for a while but when he bumped against Kenzo's new erection he jumped up and grabbed for his Dynamite-briefs. Tug of teasing war over the briefs Jiro twanged back into the far corner with them his face nothing but fear and bewilderment as pure as a baby's, breathing at last. Cowering in the corner his eyes drank up Kenzo's kicking aside the sheet his sprawling his swift hand masturbating Good Luck to your Nicky pirana alligator.

Things calmed down by and by.

Jiro made Kenzo promise to go shopping with him. Kenzo was already dressed and hanging around in the kitchen. Jiro was talking from the cupboard door as he got dressed into a beige suit and an open-necked brown shirt. The effect was altogether too suave for someone who had passed through the night and morning he'd gone through. Ashes and sackcloth would have suited the look on his face better.

Jiro also make Kenzo promise to meet him on the corner of the main intersection as he didn't want anyone to see them leaving his apartment together. Kenzo went out into the excrutiating bright sunlight by himself, blinking like someone who'd been trapped for days underground. Kenzo walked down the steps as quietly as he could but the metal rang out his departure incriminatingly. There was no one around to be seen though. Kenzo wheeled around the corner onto the main street and could almost intuit Jiro back there sighing for relief. On the corner of the hot absurd street Kenzo lit a cigarette and tapped his foot impatiently. As well as feeling rather cocky he also felt a vague but strong sort of obligation to Jiro now. Oh but what a waste of time.

A mirror in the furniture shop behind Kenzo brought Jiro's tired and sour face around the corner a second before his body. Kenzo had time to pull his face into a smile. A taxi pulled up as quickly and conveniently as a get-away car. They slid in and were off to the Ginza. So it was a day of cabs, one expensive snack after another all paid for by Kenzo's host, window-shopping, trying on clothes in places that didn't know if they were discos or boutiques, trying not to look at each other and Jiro exhorting promises from Kenzo not to say a word to Nicky about what had happened between them.

By five pm Kenzo realised he'd worked off his obligation to Jiro – that was, very simply – keeping him company on his one day off in the week. What some people will do just to get company. The last hour together was spent looking for a shoe-shop as Jiro had developed blisters. Unusual for a Japanese to walk along the Ginza in socks. They rested in a pink coffee shop and tried to eat bright pink sausages quilted over with whipped cream and sauerkraut. Then they said, or rather, nodded goodbye. As Kenzo walked towards the station he felt a large blister develop over his face from where it had gone too hard against the surface of another person's life. He avoided looking at it in the opposite window of the subway car. He wondered how long he would look like that. He knew he didn't want to repeat that experience but otherwise he tried to think of nothing, least of all of Tatsuo.

Didn't want to repeat that experience, but wanted every other. Summer too short. On Thursday Kenzo went down to Tatsuo's college and went into the computer room to compose a piece of music. How could he do that? He'd received no formal music training except what Tatsuo had shown him. But he could. He could learn quickly. Once just a familiar face in the computer room as Tatsuo's friend he was now a vengeful participant. The friendly helping hands gave him access to tapes and a piano. He pushed away at the buttons and keys. Then after an hour, having gotten nowhere, but still bursting with energy, he fled from the paraphernalia of computers and keyboards and let himself into Tatsuo's apartment to try out the piano, flute, and set of kettle drums there. Despite the acoustic opposition of the tiny hollow apartment Kenzo had, by midday, brought the instruments under his will. He didn't need or use musical notation. Fanciful, crazy, not quite himself but all of himself. He made drawings of the sounds, the edge of a 6B shading in tone and an HB extending out the structure. It all began to look like the scaffolding for some Art-Deco skyscraper but with no building inside.

So where could he put himself?

He went back to the college, thrust his papers at a technician and had him decipher and keyboard the graphite music into a form suitable for feeding the computer. The efficient machine released back out a composition with all the meat sucked off it. Only bones left. Though the technician-friend was satisfied Kenzo wasn't. Again he sped back to Tatsuo's apartment and before setting to work had a good cry out of frustration on the piano stool. If only Tatsuo would come back and help him. If only the drawings were more accurate. If only he knew how to tune the slack drumskin properly. If only, if only. As if a demon had gotten into him he tried again and made obeisant to his will the indifferent piano, flute and drum. He began to succeed. Then he grew bored. He didn't want the instruments to be so cooperative. He then created more difficulties for himself to make it all the more interesting. And then he began to succeed even more, unfortunately.

And now on Sunday. . .Ultramarine, deep, soft, high blue sky. Tinted by a cool wind, cut by the sun. Kenzo and Linda are helping to pull the roof off their friend's house in preparation for the rebuilding that is to be started tomorrow. There are five or six others as well – workmen and carpenters. The dull orange metal sheets are flung into a waiting truck below. Crowbar in hand, Linda and Kenzo prise up the roof beams which are then tossed from one worker to another down to the street. Linda swears with the best of them whenever a nail pulls her jeans. Kenzo's brow has a healthy sweat and he feels to his limits the release and thoroughness of physical exertion. More of a game than work though. The pinnacle of fun to shout and jostle and shirtless rip up the roof of a house. A respite from days that are beginning to plunge forward driverless on fixed and dead-straight rails.

The carpenters, gloved and shod in tight, knee-high leggings, are as quick as chimpanzees up down and over the scaffolding they are throwing up around the roof as the last of the beams are pulled out.

They call down Linda and Kenzo for lunch. Green tea, pickles, rice and fish packed in small wooden boxes. They eat sitting in the shade of the garden wall. They laugh and talk with their mouths full.

Linda tells Kenzo what Nicky has told her of the escapade last Monday night. Not knowing how much she knows, Kenzo, in angry self-defence, forgets his promise to Jiro to be silent and tells Linda the rest of the story. As much as pride can tell. The flippancy of the version of the story that Linda heard from Nicky disgusts Kenzo. Kenzo stabs a grain of rice in his lunch box with a chopstick. Linda has stopped laughing. Tries to change the subject to Tatsuo which as a result annoys Kenzo even more. But Kenzo doesn't want her to see his annoyance.

Linda looks up and sees one of the younger carpenters climbing up a thick pole in the scaffolding. Like a circus performer. Linda calls out everyone to look. All look up. Shirtless, sweat-band around the head, shoulder blades shining under the midday sun, the climber reaches the top of the pole, balances on one foot, calls out, laughs, then clambers back down again. Everyone claps. Kenzo saw the young carpenter topple from his perch and be speared on the crowbar protruding from the garden soil. There was blood and a wild blue sky. He likes what he thought he saw. Head tight and pounding, he is angry. But an anger he can't understand.

Forgetting. Propelled. Sunday night now. Kenzo could still taste the sliced melon and whisky the hostess in the bar had coaxed upon him and Misa. They turned down the suddenly dropping street. A sandwich shop, a coin laundry, a coffee shop. They passed by those sentries and suddenly vanished in front of the footsteps behind them into a Love Hotel as there was nowhere else to go. The hotel woman led them up the turning narrow tower stairs, mirrors throwing their reflections at every step to a room near the top of Sunday night. The window showed them the grey battleship sides of the other buildings. Pick-up Misa turned on the taps and the water crashed into the huge cracked bath. Kenzo jumped onto the bed and switched the air-conditioning on.

Kenzo and Misa connected on the bed, kissed, then disconnected. They stood up. As if daring each other they boldly undressed in the middle of the room which suddenly felt as wide as a city square with them standing as naked as sacrifices on a platform. Kenzo felled Misa to the bed just under the gaze of the wall mirror. It was quick. Misa's breath was pushed up under his collarbones as he came. Could smell nothing but the dank rich odour of semen so strong you could almost grow things in it. Misa slipped away, fell asleep under Kenzo's after caresses. Kenzo linked him completed him with soft touches noticing he was only ordinary but somehow so beautiful to Kenzo. Misa's legs and hips just right. A bit of hair up the shins. Smooth equal planes of belly and chest, good lines showing where they went under each other. Nipples even in sleep soft one second then tight screws coming out the next between Kenzo's fingers so far away from sleep. Sleep a waste. Awake he needed information from looking to store away in the sleep library for the next night for a rainy day. For when he can no longer touch or be touched.

Kenzo kept compulsively touching Misa as lightly as possible in disbelief as if never satisfied that Misa was human that he himself was human. No proof enough. Until Misa woke of his own accord.

Into the bathroom splashing and brushing his teeth for an epoch. Kenzo meanwhile lay as still as naked as possible, thinking and not thinking.

Then the room wound Misa back into itself, a damp blue towel around his hips. A slit up the side. Rocking on the balls of his feet getting down something. Kenzo had already folded and hung up his clothes for him. Misa appreciated that above all. Kenzo went around the back smiling and held Misa from behind. His penis in between Misa's buttocks persuaded him forward to the worn black velvet window where they looked out. Standing as if on a space balcony rushing at light speeds in all directions but always only overlooking the sour smog and zinging neons of Shinjuku. An eternity at the window.

Making them fall back on the bed, pulling the little blue towel aside sheer nudity blood going faster. Lip and teeth. Long unbroken licks from ankle to chin. An emotion growing in Kenzo an unbearable inarticulation until hands and skin going hotter white stuff leaping out again. Misa's face at the last minute went like a pup's or a kitten's, something frantic from behind his open mouth and eyes opening but never enclosing or quite reaching Kenzo. Kenzo stroked Misa's hair to sleep and Misa was mercifully dragged back under. Kenzo could watch him again asleep. Kenzo grew like a forest around him. He surrounded to protect him. Misa slept as small as an animal in Kenzo's arms. No matter to where Misa turned in sleep he was always drawn back. His tongue licking his lips in sleep, crackling in Kenzo's ear. Deep pore perfumes in his body melting and coming out. Stubble as fine mauve powder on his chin. Kenzo took in everything and hoarded it all so it would never die. Never be flesh.

In the eerie wonderful morning Kenzo woke guiltily having dozed at his post. But nothing had happened. The whole room and its contents were still safe inside him. Though Misa kept his eyes closed his altered breathing told Kenzo he too was awake. Misa waited on the other side of the door of his body. Misa gradually opened out at the polite insistence of Kenzo's hands. The white centre of him came out again up Kenzo's arm and side. Almost simultaneously Kenzo was ejecting white loops and buds coming down in loose gob relaxations Kenzo almost relaxed, a kite on water, biting only soft water.

He let Misa go and wash. The sound Kenzo had kept hearing at 19 intervals during the night – that of a one-legged giant going up and down the muffled tower stairs – had finally stopped. He could extract his earplugs. His watch and ring scratched as he rearranged them on the low bureau. Misa came back three drops of gold water on his hip as he leaned over. Kenzo was pretending to be asleep. Kenzo's turn now Misa caressed him and slowly brushed his hair with his brush, as if the world would never end.

They tumbled down the endless mirror stairs to arrive into their own shoes, to turn the heavy glass doors around onto the dry summer street. No face there was more than paper. The great grey streets cleaving their way to the horizon would've been frightening if not so fantastic then. Kenzo and Misa were still so inured on small flesh-textured spaces the odourless buildings appeared as negating as they really always were.

They hugged close together as canoeists going down a canyon river. Their stomachs rescued them from obliteration by demanding the small area of a coffee shop in which to be satisfied. A waitress bent the elongated bronze spout of a coffee pot over their cups. The other small details of sugar, cigarette lighter and a flower crowded forward to reassure them against the city. The smiling waitress poured out another cup for them. But what was destroyed the minute they had orbited through the past-tense glass doors could never be recreated. Going to a lunch place later on they saw some birds in a cage in the centre of a department store. Kenzo and Misa pitied those birds and couldn't stop looking at them as they took shelter in an elevator going down.

And Kenzo thought – I am screaming so quietly no one can hear me.

Glancing over her bookshelves, Harriet is checking to see how many books she's lent out, and how many she's borrowed. She always does this before visiting anyone's house. She sucks thoughtfully on the bit of blue-vein cheese in her mouth.

She's got a good mind to start up her own little library card system to keep a check, once and for all, on the inflow and outflow of books through her shelves. Harriet is her own best secretary. The neatly labelled and arranged folders of lecture notes testify to that. Also in proof of her wise planning into the future is the pile of scholarship and research grant application forms waiting to be filled out on her desk.

Anyway, she thinks, to butter Linda up in preparation for getting off her those new books on Zen Linda bought just the other day, she'll take her a jar of home-made pickled vegetables. Admittedly the jar's half empty, Harriet having picked the eyes out of it, but then again, it really is the thought that counts.

'It certainly is a beautiful day,' Linda says to no one but herself, as she climbs a little farther up the coast road around Izu peninsula, a hundred or so kilometres from Tokyo.

This road goes climbing and falling around the whole length of the peninsula. Linda doesn't have any intention of walking the whole length though. Just a few kilometres, then back to her friend's hut in the mountains for the night. Back to Toyko and the grind tomorrow.

On the spur of the moment Linda had asked Kenzo to come too, but then he rang back later to say he couldn't come after all.

Climbing the steep road to the top of the rise has given Linda a healthy sweat, not the nervous acidic sweat worked up in the Tokyo summer bustle. So good to be away from that metropolis for a while. Linda can already feel the tonic effect of the open sky and good air.

As she walks, when she lifts her head, she can see the land and seascape present itself more and more panoramically. A different kind of panorama to that of the Australian coastline. The involved and the intimate coastline of Japan – in the bottom of every fold and tuck of it a collection of at least a few houses, gable to gable, with four or five fishing boats pulled up high, drying out on the shingles.

No great surf crashes on the pebble beaches here, the continental shelf being quite narrow and deep off the Izu peninsular. There are few cliffs on this coastline, the mountains and hills just rather gently dropping their slopes down into the sea. The rich green of the vegetation goes right down to the sea and is lined with white there.

The country is geologically young, hence its volcanoes and hot springs. Izu is famous for its spas and hot springs these days. In Shogunate days Izu was an untamed wilderness inhabited only by bandits, a few fishermen, and exiled trouble-makers from the Imperial court in Kyoto.

Linda has finally reached the top of the rise. She straightens up and surveys what she's been so looking forward to seeing. The vista is not so breathtaking but the sea and the sky seem very soothing in their drowsy closeness and warmth. All is calm and quiet, the horizon soft and hazy. On the seemingly not so distant horizon the sunlight is thin and lemon pale. The summer colours of sea and sky are always more muted than the wind-scoured, brilliant cobalts and turquoises of winter. It was worth coming here, Linda thinks as she feels the edges of her body haze out. Her nerves, untangled now, billow easily like silk thread under water. She stretches and leans back on her hips in the warm sunshine. . . A very faint earth-shudder goes through the path beneath her. It is as if the earth, like flesh, has given a little shiver in the sunshine. . . Unalarmed, hardly noticing it, Linda walks on a little farther. She takes several deep breaths. She thinks how much she loves the outdoors. One disadvantage of living in Japan for her is that it is difficult to really get out of doors, the cities here encompassing you as they do. In Australia, Linda often went swimming, riding and skiing. In Japan those activities are so expensive and crowded-out that the effort of getting to the point of actually doing them exhausts you before you've even started.

Just then, coming into view, a small boat has pushed out from a village inlet beneath the hill. A sailing boat, only one man at the tiller. Linda watches it as it slowly ducks though the slightly breaking waves. . .

Peering at it for a while then losing interest Linda thinks again how she'd love to be able to do more swimming and riding. Lucky Tatsuo, swimming to his heart's content in the warm waters of the Okinawan islands. She wouldn't mind being there with him. And maybe for not just the swimming. Did that curious look he often gave her still mean anything in particular, Linda wonders, still sure that he's just as aware of her as a woman as he is of her as a person. Maybe, she thinks, she still wouldn't mind some kind of little fling with him. But no, she reconsiders, he's too aware of his handsomeness. Linda feels she couldn't be bothered playing up to that ego. He doesn't seem to give Kenzo any trouble though, Kenzo somehow having been able to blunt the worst of Tatsuo's conceit. And he wouldn't need to give Kenzo a bad time, Linda thinks defensively to herself. Kenzo is very special to her. Something about him – she doesn't know exactly what – his eagerness or his vulnerability, has worked an influence over her. Anyway, she doesn't consider it important to be able to put her finger on exactly what attracts her to him. She doesn't like trying to lay bare the every ligament of her relationships now. That kind of dog-chasing-its-tail analysis she had more than enough of back in her uni. days in Sydney. Everybody there wanted a reason for everything, and an explanation for the reason as well. Everybody thought they were amateur psychoanalysts. If not that, they tried to pull you apart with their fanatic cults and therapies and self-help groups. One of the reasons she came to Japan was to get away from that modern narcissism. Weary of that, she is by no means under any illusions about Japanese relationships. Over her three years in Japan so far she's had a number of relationships with Japanese men, including one unhappy living-together relationship with her last lover. That's no more now. Sick of demanding sexual attachments she has happily found the opposite swing of the pendulum in her platonic relationship with Kenzo. Linda likes how she can be a kind of older sister to Kenzo without having to pay that usual price with Japanese men – becoming their maid and second mother. For fortunately Kenzo is homosexual. Thus outside the usual male-female roles, Linda can relax with Kenzo and get down to just being friends.

Buddhism is their main meeting-ground, for Linda off and on toys with the idea of maybe one day becoming a Zen nun. It rather troubles her that Kenzo lately doesn't seem to want to talk about Buddhism as much as he used to. He seems restless. . .

Back in May, when Tatsuo and Kenzo become lovers, she was initially amazed that a novice Zen priest could have a male lover. But, as Tatsuo pointed out to her, in Japanese history male homosexuality was never so very incompatible with Zen or even with Samurai. Many priests and warriors had lovers, Tatsuo explained: only contact with women was thought to be weakening. (Though of course, in the Zen sect Kenzo's family belongs to, it is the tradition for priests to marry and beget children.)

Linda laughed at Tatsuo then, thinking he was bending history to his rationale a little too conveniently, but then she just accepted Kenzo's and Tatsuo's relationship for what it was. They have been grateful to her for that.

Linda smiles and squints at the horizon, thinking of the time she and Tatsuo went to the gay disco in Shinjuku in the period when Tatsuo and Kenzo were still just friends. (She'd met Tatsuo through Kenzo.) With the boys sashaying and shimmying around them Linda got drunk enough to start teasing Tatsuo, and she said that everything in Japan, including the penises, was too small. As she might have predicted, that kind of joke soon began to wear interestingly thin with Tatsuo who, being proud and sexy Tatsuo, was not going to admit to any small penis. They danced away all the wilder, trying to out-shimmy the other. Tatsuo was loose-jointedly athletic in his grubby sandshoes. Linda began dancing her way around him to confuse his steps and the other couples clapped her on and made her and Tatsuo the centre of attention. Tatsuo quickly became 'tired' and said he was going out for a bowl of noodles, and if Linda wanted to come too she could, but if she wanted to stay and make a show of herself then. . .

When they had finished their noodles at about one am, they decided to look at their watches to discover, with fake surprise, that they had missed their last trains home. So, they had nothing to do for the next five hours but talk and wonder in the back of their minds who was going to ask whom back to his or her apartment, and for not only a drink. That moment never came, and actually, later, on thinking back to that night, they were both rather glad they hadn't said anything. It could have ruined the happily threesome friendship with Kenzo. So instead, they just talked the night away in coffee shops and then when the sun came up, not wanting to go home yet, they wandered around the ash-coloured and dead-neon Shinjuku looking for somewhere to have some breakfast. Both wanting toast but only Chinese restaurants seeming to be open, Tatsuo said, 'Okay then, let's have Chinese toast!' They both then laughed themselves sick and while staggering about, holding each other up, they did then see a coffee shop which had toast.

Still not altogether certain that the other wasn't going to say 'Well, why don't we go back to my place,' they ate and talked and laughed until they would've been too tired for sex anyway. At eight am they finally went home – to their respective beds. In the following weeks the potential problem of what stance to adopt sexually to the other was solved when Tatsuo's relationship with Kenzo became sexual. Both Linda and Tatsuo felt relieved but were all the same just a little disappointed that the delicious tension had diminished from their relationship. It has never completely gone however. . .

Linda now laughs quietly, staring out at the horizon. That precious little twinkle in Tatsuo's eyes. She savours it. . .

The sun has made her sleepy now, and so she sits down on her haunches in the grass by the side of the road. She feels faintly tired. Remembering something, she looks out, scanning the sea for an object. There it is – the little sailing boat. It is far away, heading straight out to sea to God only knows where. Linda stares after the boat, shielding her eyes from the sun, happy for the boat's setting out. Then she feels a strange vague sympathy, a slight apprehension for the man at the tiller, so alone. She imagines herself as him. She marvels at the expert hand one must need to keep sail trimmed or slack, rope taut and tiller steady in fine balance against the wind and current and whatever unexpected fish, flotsam or storm that might spring up. It seems like the sailing of some Ulysses. . . I wish you well, Linda calls softly in her heart.

And it calls softly. Dreaming ceasing dreaming and. . . Tatsuo morning. Rubbing out of his eyes what he'd seen while sleeping, rubbing his arms padding over to crackle the blinds to see the mark of sunlight on the Okinawan sky. Sunlight cracking out of an ice-cube. Another day. Coming out of his body another day further away from his birth. The snow melting a little more he rubs one shin against the other in the shower while splashing his brown skin rubbing thousands of cells off his face into the bath towel.

Morning unbelievable morning another day closer to muscular

perfection. The body remembering itself after a long night amazed at what it remembers. It flexes and relaxes. And preens in the mirror combing back hair. Opening the windows wider and wider for Hotel View: palms Banana leaf on Blue Sky the sun marking out the smooth waves on the smooth beach sand in the thongs he stands in an atoll of perfection creation pure unrefined youthfulness. Not yet twenty-five from when the inner clock starts losing time.

Out on the beach now – the sea the sky hailing him remembering his body singing its anthem remembering the way he marks the waves the way he stands so still for the sky to decorate his shoulders. The sun wants to open his skin itself and see all the juice sacs within. All nature makes way for him, claims him, falls behind him in his wake his simple clean shadow the mark of bathing trunks barely visible.

He arches. A sudden crease between his shoulder blades he dives the creak in the pier going right down the post minutely to the fish on the clear bottom nibbling nibbling forever. Cleaving out. The waves go cleaving to the horizon which parts. A little. Thought about Kenzo and Linda and Tokyo and changing his ways, oh to be able to greet them now and sing so loud the ticking of the clock can't be heard.

For it's already lunchtime. Tabasco sauce on pizza quizzical face in the bottom of the glass. There'd been a woman on the beach as brown as he she reminded him of Linda who is ineluctably associated with Kenzo. Aah Kenzo. I know where you are but you are not here. The pagoda of loneliness goes tier by tier into the bluest sky. Trapped up there calling down to Kenzo. The memory of the body tinkling like a lost bell in the mountains under never melting snow. It will never die. Never melt. The wanting to nuzzle in his armpit. Wanting to rub hair against hair. Where is Kenzo? Been away too long. But had to get away from that furnace relationship for a while. A cigarette burning until it falls off the edge of the ashtray. A body burning slowly. Been a celibate the whole time here changing his ways changing for love maybe. Keeping himself for another body which will make Tatsuo forget his terror of losing his hair his teeth his virility. The tender arrogance of virility. The disgustingness of old age. He is so disgusted he returns beating the air with his towel to the beach stamping ground where he is again –

Tatsuo in full leaf. His blood the sharpest juices his semen the most stinging sap. Must be mirrored by the beach. Not a cloud the sky must pity him, the sunlight in his bones murmuring with pity now as he strikes down a wave and yet another wave until he has learnt what a wave is and becomes a wave and races up the beach of his own life and dissolves, its ambition for a natural death having been satisfied.

. . .Swimming under water again old age and death and loneliness can be drowned. He would put death off like a medical appointment. Puts thinking about it off until he breaks surface again and then after all it has gone. For when it doesn't hurt you forget about it.

. . .Scuffing through the dry sand the trouble with being by yourself you think about death too much – he mutters to himself but hoping Kenzo and Linda will hear and sympathise. He puts a shell to his ear. He hears Tokyo. It wants him back. It summons him to take his place again in the anti-death generation city. So let's all get old together he mutters under his breath but really screaming down the infinities between the grains of sand. The sun touches his shoulder. A soothing gesture at first but then it touches him everywhere leering and jeering and perverting. Mauled, he takes refuge under a beach umbrella. Ruffled feathers cooling down, a long straw in the cocktail light softly hatching out of the ice-cube. He is a bruised god soothing his flesh with suntan oil. Persuading his priceless rich skin it is immortal. He is noticing the line of his penis under nylon a line crooning and telling itself the story of the minutes it spent in Kenzo's mouth. The story becomes a Legend a Myth and Chant a Mass a Beatific Ecstasy separated from the universe by only a millimetre of nylon. It gets a little bigger. Tatsuo puts down his glass and looks around. But no one saw.

. . .The shadows lengthen along the beach. The creature in the shade dozes. A small sweat moustache. The Forces want to play with him again so they wake him up – The Beach Woman wriggles past again treading down the lifeless sand. Stirring up Tatsuo's cells again to storm in the teacup his tongue reddening his lips thinking of women, not men. Thinking of Linda for example. Must marry. Must procreate. Must plough his seed into some woman's body – soon. Soon must make mirrors down through the ages to reflect from afar but ever so clearly his perfect biology. His knife-sharp body. The wonder of it still echoing in the valleys of a hundred years time. Music and computers not enough. There are easier ways to win immortality. Aaah but no use crying over the spilt milk of his seed on Kenzo's body. It cannot be avoided. He will continue to do so and experience the old familiar ecstatic regret.

Regret, regret, the sun slants pulling down streamers of yellow and orange. They slowly snap. The day is departing The Beach Woman gone only the men singing now pulling in the nets. Pulling in his body retrieving his body the sea and sky are forgetting his body Tatsuo must try and remember something to keep existing – But it's the wrong thing. Here it comes the symbolism of death and fleeting youth in Japanese history – the falling cherry blossoms the melting snow the wilting red maple leaves. Stars being switched on now the circular shade melting into night shade, dew tinkling on the sand the beach umbrella folding its petals.

Dinner time. Another meal to be mountain-climbed. Down on the other side at last electric light going to sleep in another ice-cube. Tomb. In the bar. Impatient for the Beach Woman's shell earrings and bra-dress to glide their way in tonight but she doesn't come. Another man another bar. Tatsuo grumpily throws down some coins on the counter and drags his feet upstairs. Upstairs sleazy hotel room run the bath peel of skin Tokyo calls Dick Whittington. The great decision in the bath to send a telegram to say he's coming back. Wait for me. Open your arms Linda and Kenzo and . . .

The warm water laps his shining muscles praising the well-honed edges and planes. Feeling his leg at close quarters he is disgusted again. His poor beautiful leg doomed to go as soft and rotten and sour as banana one day. Old age calls from the mirror – You loll so easily in the bath but the water is heated melted snow and cherry blossom petals float around you whose points will wither and crinkle up like red maple stars. Get out of the bath. Look in the mirror. Tatsuo does so dripping nudity every cell in the universe before his eyes struggling for life and nothing but life. It's too much to bear . . .

The snubbed mirror watches him as he goes into the bedroom to telephone the telegram office. His back to the mirror on his heel.

Changing changing twisting off course headed towards derailment any sudden future curve in events won't be able to take his propulsion. Kenzo haywiring. His head programmed for Zen but playing video neon games. Cross-circuiting information terminals. Modern Japan. Tokyo rebuffing making him think he hasn't known any best or worst of anything after all. Kenzo lighter than air escaping beyond air, wanting, wanting everything and more and more again of life. The desperation of the organic. His experiences which do not satisfy him. He is dislocated. A piece of lost property. A star fixed telescopes deny. Contextless. Confusion and utter clarity of purpose the one. He is simply occurring without his knowledge. He is as innocent as a stone which cannot be blamed for tripping someone.

Gas gripped in a bottle. A bird in a shrinking cage. A being gripped in a body, no escape. You twist for your life grabbing at air on the end of a gangplank summer ending beneath your feet for who wants to become a monk?

3 Linda's apartment is quite large by Tokyo standards. Potentially comfortable, it is however very untidy – a mirror strewn with the materialised pieces of Linda's strewn psyche. The apartment has a hazed, washed-out, dirty pastel fluorescent look, as if the months of unventilated cigarette and incense smoke have greyed the original wall and carpet colours. Her study room is inhabited by rows of unread books, dishes of sticky evaporating soya sauce and a huge unsteady bookcase. With its simple tatami lines ruined by the pieces of scattered plastic bric-a-brac, the proportions of the sleeping room are just as unbalanced as those of the study room. The unaired futon is permanently spread on the floor, with the pillow dress-circled around by filled ashtrays, burst packets of biscuits, odds and ends of make-up, alarm clocks, Zen books and the various felt pens for marking them with. Linda's kitchen is crowded with fruit blenders and coffee pots. The kitchen carpet is stained with tea and miso. And under the rubber mat in the sink there is a black sludge of frying pan oil and tea leaf mulch.

Linda, however, is not as dirty as her apartment would suggest. She spends much time showering and deodorising her actual person; it's just that she's so busy running off to temples, skiing and calligraphy classes she simply hasn't 'the time for housework'.

But the apartment has just had one of its rare tidyings this morning. For Harriet is here, the tidily short as a hospital matron Harriet, the Harriet whose own rooms' cleanliness screams at the any stray hair on her immaculate floors. On stepping in the door half an hour ago Harriet's eyes photoed the whole still untidy apartment like those of a detective on the scene of a crime; it's all filed away to somehow one day be used against Linda's credibility as a person.

In contrast to her impeccabilities however, Harriet's appearance is insolently casual, sensually ugly, with a burst of hair like ginger-gold rubber bands. Being in the same room as the blonde and nordically fresh-looking Linda makes her look even more drastic.

Coffee now on the table between them, Harriet leans back, pretending she hasn't noticed how Linda served the coffee spilt in the saucer or the biscuit more crumbs than biscuit. The conversation has been about Kenzo – 'No, I didn't know Kenzo's been going to discos lately,' Harriet says with great curiosity, leaning forward, the duchess in the pantomine, always interested.

But Linda didn't really want to bring that up. She doesn't know why she mentioned discos. Now she could be drawn out unprepared by Harriet which can easily be done, given Harriet's knack of extracting information.

'So . . .?' Harriet responds again, even more interested.

'Well,' Linda continues, aware of having trapped herself, 'only now and then you know.'

'How often is "now and then"?'

'About once a month,' Linda lies.

'Why does he want to be going to discos all of a sudden?'

'I don't know. I took him . . . With a friend.'

'Where? The gay one?'

'Oh, in Shinjuku. You know.'

'No I don't know. Which one? I might have been there.'

Indeed she might have. Zen has never prevented Harriet from having her 'night on the town': Zen explores.

'Where most of the discos are in Shinjuku . . .' Linda vaguely answers, looking around the room for a new book to look at which will hopefully attract Harriet's eyes to it and then happily cause the subject to be changed.

Harriet has always taken an impersonally professional interest in Kenzo. Linda got to know Kenzo through Harriet, Harriet and Linda themselves having met at a Zen centre in Tokyo. Up until last January Linda was attending a monthly 'Zen temple weekend' for foreigners organised by an American novice nun. At the time Harriet was already a Deshi (disciple-student) to Kenzo's father the head-priest at Kenzo's family's temple in Chiba-prefecture. One weekend Harriet took Linda along to Kenzo's temple, partly out of a desire to prove to Linda her temple was better than the American woman's. Linda met Kenzo there after lunch. Though Harriet had no particular friendship with Kenzo, Linda quickly warmed to him, and Kenzo invited Linda to meditate regularly at the temple. (Harriet was not to be too happy about having introduced competition into the temple.)

Watching Kenzo and Linda talking together Harriet considered the stories she'd heard about Kenzo from one of the temple's old retainers. Apparently Kenzo as an infant had nearly died from an infection of the spinal fluid; then in childhood he had been unruly and often disobedient: when put in a corner to meditate his misbehaviour away he'd just sing or pick holes in the wall before him. There were no smackings in Zen temples, so Kenzo found himself enduring several very cold and prolonged 'meditations'. And the old servant had other stories as well – about Kenzo's family's past: in the sixteenth century there was someone who became a Christian and who was subsequently crucified; later on there was someone who helped make one of the first Japanese-English dictionaries; then there was a highly distinguished Gagaku musician; and in the early 1900s two members of Kenzo's father's side of the family went mad and ran amok . . .

So from a distance Harriet observed Kenzo and Linda talking, and she found herself resolving to keep the stories to herself.

Still looking at the books now, Linda thinks how repulsive they seem, hard and edged as they are, stacked up against her weakened frame of mind, which is trying to defend Kenzo to herself. She must protect him from Harriet's curiosity. For he is part of herself. He attractively embodies the quests and conflicts Linda herself feels. She likes her idols flawed so they don't embarrass her own deficiencies. Seeing firstly the good in others, she regards herself as basically a good person, her goodness admittedly being partly an insecure safeguard against reprisals from the world if she were to ever be very bad. Mere ordinary goodness though, doesn't seem to be quite enough. Linda sees Kenzo as possibly being able to demonstrate to her the Zen way to true goodness. Harriet, with her overawing, shaming technical knowledge of Zen provides Linda with a filling-in of the gaps Kenzo leaves. Linda, a very late twentieth-century girl, if just a little more insecure, vulnerable and lost, or humourless, would be easy material for any one of the more extreme, Moonie-style cults.

But Zen is enough.

Harriet is still waiting for Linda to continue about Kenzo's discos. Linda looks up and almost flinches. Harriet has that look on her face she gets when she is about to tap something with impatience. She hates vagueness. But Linda is saved – Harriet suddenly screams. She has just seen something that tickles her fancy in the book on the coffee table she has been all the while reading out of the corner of her eye. She now hee hees with smug delight. (It was probably a dry joke in an article about some precious academic absurdity.)

Linda laughs too. She feels suddenly endeared to Harriet. Harriet had to scream, so she did. No social inhibitions about her. A scream out of Harriet is never all that surprising though. A woman with such a galleon-hull of a bottom and tumble-weed hair has enough harsh comedy about her to make any scream seem a wholly natural consequence of her physical virulence. But is she the kind of person you can really open your heart to? Linda feels that if she did open up she could imagine Harriet fastidiously cutting the crusts off what was told her and pushing them to one side in preparation for a making of a sandwich out of the rest. And how Harriet would summarise how you felt would bamboozle you into believing it even though you knew it wasn't true. Then you'd have yourself surrounded by the dotted lines of Harriet's theories, and be coloured in.

'That's that Nakahara book isn't it?' – Harriet squints over at the bookcase, at which Linda has been absent-mindedly staring, Linda having forgotten she's been trying to look for a certain book to make Harriet change the subject and stop quizzing about Kenzo.

'. . Mm. Yes. *Eastern Thinking*. You've read it haven't you?'

'Probably . . ,' Harriet mumbles, now standing at the bookcase, squinting at the Nakahara book as if trying to outstare it. Any book having the audacity to sit on a shelf perhaps unread by Harriet she takes as a very personal challenge. She pulls it out and flips through it as if it were some disreputable cheap thriller. 'I've read it.' She snaps it shut in disgust, but all the same, when she sits down again, keeps it within hand's reach so it can be referred to if the conversation might happen to take a turn in its direction.

Linda has had a lively game going with Harriet for months: she's been trying to buy a Buddhism book Harriet hasn't read. So far she hasn't succeeded.

'Some parts of it are okay,' pronounces Harriet, referring to the book, 'for the general reader. But a lot of things in it are off.'

'Oh, I thought it was very interesting,' says Linda.

'Yes, I would have imagined that . . .' Harriet says, suddenly intensely bored, giving the room a severe glance, picturing herself at home – immaculate at her own desk surveying neat folders, Sanskrit dictionaries and well-filled fountain pens.

Usually at a moment like this Linda sensibly disappears to make another cup of coffee to leave Harriet alone, but this time she doesn't. Instead she starts practising Chinese characters on a pad on her lap. She knows that at any moment Harriet will crane over and tell her her stroke-order is wrong. Harriet's been studying Japanese for years. She can take notes directly from Japanese source materials. Linda goes on writing out the Kanji anyway, marvelling to herself at what an efficient housekeeper Harriet is of her life. There is Harriet pulling in the harvests with bright machinery while Linda has to push an old plough through to produce anything at all. Harriet's fields have been well fertilised with research grant money; Linda has to work hard at teaching to pay for her courses in Buddhism. Harriet teaches too, but only enough for folio-edition book-buying money.

Linda's pen seems to be getting bogged down in the Kanji. She feels depressed. Looking up a little, she considers the steel ankles of the chair across the narrow room. There above the chair is a mirror on the wall, the small square cut out of the centre of it filled with a picture of a Kabuki actor. Next to the mirror is a poster of the poutingly white-faced 'Onnagata' himself. Everything is faintly yellow, as if the smog had gotten into the room.

It all seems so unfair; here is Harriet doing her Masters in Buddhism and myself doing what?, Linda wonders – piffling and squandering myself away on various nothings. Look at that nose of Harriet's – ever on the scent of trails that may bring her closer to fame and fortune. It is true though, despite her bias of passing self-pity, what Linda thinks of Harriet's ambitiousness. Harriet does want to become the Catherine the Great of the empire of Buddhist studies. The new breed of relentless Australian. She'll set them talking in the universities one day with some authoritative work of scholarship. Just to be able to get an essay out of it, she'll do the marathon meditation with the best of them in the meditation hall, in the unheated dead of winter. She is already a Deshi to Kenzo's father. The day at the temple when she was presented with her Deshi's smock by Kenzo's father during a special ceremony for which she had gathered all her friends as witnesses, she was as gloatingly jubilant as the girl who catches the bride's bouquet. Now that the capricious novelty of it has worn off though, the smock is not even looked at.

34 | But yes, Harriet's book is going to succeed for she has the

ambition of a Borgia. She's a carnivore. She chews her way through books, people and ideas, and neatly ejects what she doesn't need. Linda can just picture Harriet in a Sydney bookstore – bald, resolutely short in her brown robes, and signing copies of one of her bestsellers on Buddhism – *101 Zen Kitchen Recipes* – one of the attractions for Harriet about Zen being the tasty food served up in the temples. It is indeed delicious. Harriet likes her food, her cushions and her front seats at Kabuki.

'But what was that you were going to say about Kenzo?' Harriet suddenly asks, interested in the world again.

'Oh nothing.' Linda gets up to make more coffee to take her shameful face into the kitchen. Linda tells herself that, despite her usual intimidated awe of Harriet, she would've told Harriet to her face what she'd been thinking, if Harriet had asked her what she really thought of her Zen. Linda peers vacantly at the gas flame under the kettle, regretting now what she's been thinking about Harriet, thinking of how very big-hearted Harriet can often be. (Harriet once offered her a large loan when she thought Linda was hard-up, and helped her with her essays for her Buddhist studies course.) She feels she could have had a decent conversation with Harriet then, talked unselfconsciously about Kenzo and her feelings about Zen and clarified herself through Harriet, but she didn't; she was too timidly vague, too self-defensive.

'Do you need any help?' Harriet perfunctorily calls from the study room. Her eyes are narrowed with intense suspicion and curiosity, her mouth a mere slit the more involved she is becoming with the magazine on Oriental thought she is reading.

'. . . No,' Linda murmurs trying not to sound to mournful. It's an effort. She is sinking into herself, trying to grasp familiar, reassuring things. They evade her. So she must defend Kenzo and herself from the world. Kenzo is no bird to be brought down by one of the arrows of conversation. Let him stay in the corners and caves. Let him change as he does through Linda's mind like seawater to cloud to rain. Her affection for him is probably the only real thing she has. She wants to keep the growing space Kenzo occupies in her life as free of her untidiness as possible. Free of her insecurities. She feels she is one of those moths that live just for a season and then die to be replaced by others indistinguishable from her. She cannot accept how her hands are empty of the weapons that hold the future at bay, master and utilise it. The ambitious and coolly masculine way Harriet deals with her future unnerves Linda though that is how she wishes she could do it too . . .

The whole nebulous greyness of her life encroaches in like a tide and, gazing helplessly at distant, capable Harriet on her rock, Linda sinks as if in swamp sand.

The kettle boils. She'll let it boil. How she just wants to talk to Harriet, put her head on her lap, anything. But no. Harriet climbs up your words like a ladder to get down only what she wants. And Harriet always makes you say things you don't want to say; somehow, miraculously, cunningly, making you conveniently agree or disagree with what Harriet thinks. Harriet shapes everything so it can be stepped over. She'd hold her skirts high if she ever were to stand in Linda's puddle.

Staring at the flame under the kettle, Linda decides no – she won't say anything to Harriet.

It is getting dark now. She will have to turn the lights on soon.

It is now evening. Kenzo has shut himself up for days with his composition. He feels that the fine balance between mastering the music and being mastered by it could now be jeopardised by his excessive close quarters with the music. He feels if he spent another day alone with the piano, flute and drum the balance of his being would be destroyed. The dexterity that is required to be able to walk the tightrope of creating is mortally tiring. He must now remove himself outside and let the room simmer down of its own accord. The fire of the shadow of his energy will blaze up in his absence but on his return all will be clean and purified again. But now he is moodily empty. The sound of his shadow's footsteps is jarringly loud on the floorboards. His one shadow multiplies into a crowd and threatens to storm him, challenge his authority and call for his exile or suicide. It is unnerving to stand alone on a high balcony before that mob of himself. Kenzo must placate and quell himself, tell himself there are other existences and alternatives available to him outside this stuffy room, must open the windows to show himself that we are all orbiting around that sun out there and not just around a piano.

So Kenzo now longs for the street. The rich multiplicity of faces echoing down plate-glass windows and the extraordinary purposefulness of bikes swerving, cars going in the one direction together, eyes lifting all together to see a banner waving above a department store shall restore him. He wants to be filled to the brink again and let his shadow sink as a dark stone out of sight into this city, for this evening at least.

Linda goes back to the telephone. She tries Kenzo's number again but no answer, then Harriet's. The receiver rings in Linda's damp palm. It rings for a long time. Another receiver on the other side of Tokyo is finally picked up.

'Hello. Is that you Harriet?'

The front of a train all velocity can't turn around to see what is thrusting it. Tokyo night High-Tech super-dazzle. Neon rain, neon lighting, neon fountains meteors. Electricity thirsty slaking the black night. Super-city megalopolis neon ice. Neon frost gripping the city. Neon rainbows inside the camera, the computer, the filament which is Tokyo in a soft rain. A soft rain falling on the footbridge in Shibuya, where twenty-eight days ago Kenzo's life was transfixed without his even knowing it.

Kenzo sits at the bar of the 'Men's Hotel' drinking down beers to make himself drunk as quickly as possible. A pain in the head to douse. Chinese goldfish with balloon air sacs wobbling on the sides of their bodies are drifting up and down in their aquarium. The barman pushes a tiny basket of minute silver-foil-wrapped salami tidbits closer towards Kenzo. Only one other person is here – his mouth attached to his glass like the goldfish's is to the side of the tank, vibrating now a moment as a faint earth tremor passes under.

'Why not so many people are here,' the barman explains, 'is because it's Wednesday night.' Kenzo feels raw and young to need an explanation like that. He is becoming more and more nervous and excited. Fed up with waiting in bars and discos to pick someone up or be picked up he came here – the tawdry last resort. But he is putting off the moment for as long as possible when he'll have to go upstairs. So he makes conversation about the goldfish with the barman. The barman tells him about each fish, but Kenzo is not listening. He has fallen silent, thinking: Damn it! Priests – armchair humans.

Pushing back his stool and going upstairs along the carpeted corridor Kenzo sees a foreigner skulking in a corner. Even foreign diplomats are said to come here for their pleasure as well as blacks who, because of their blackness and despite their reputations for juicy fat penises, do not find too many pleasure-partners in colour-conscious Japan.

Down the corridor, Kenzo pushes open a sliding shoji door. His eyes blink to make out shapes in the darkness inside. But it is rude to stand at the door gaping too long so he must enter, pick his way over treacherously soft and rustling bedding to plant himself, as aimless now as a piece of washed-up flotsam, on the end of a futon. He has forgotten why he came here, forgotten the unendurable desire to touch and be touched he had while hurrying towards this place. He feels like a little boy now. Never been in a place like this before. A hotbed of clap, crabs or worse? But the feel of the cool white quilt is soothing to the sweaty palm of his hand and the shaded red lamps begin to promise something.

Accustomed to the darkness now he can make out six or seven bodies lying to his right and left in varying stages of emergence from their yukata robes. Some are entwined in embrace. The bodies lie as still as snakes only to suddenly whip up, retie yukata cords and stagger out of the room. The heavy dank silence of the room is broken suddenly by the sound of licking and sucking. Kenzo stares in alarm at the pair of dim bodies that are making that sound. He resists, because he knows he must, an urge to rush out of the creeping room, get dressed and go home. He would never forgive himself if he left like that. This experience, he feels, must be penetrated to the bone by his curiosity. So there is nothing to do but lie down and see what happens.

Lying down gingerly he tries to relax. It becomes almost comfortable lying there on the soft clean bedding near the floor as figures loom and recede in the further darkness. Every now and then the door slides open like the moon shifting off the sun in an eclipse. Out of the blaze of light a figure descends. And lies down close to Kenzo. In the darkness Kenzo feels his mouth smiling, sneering and laughing ever so slightly and quietly.

Suddenly his robe is thrust apart and his soft penis seized by a hand. His penis could belong to another body for all the connection Kenzo feels with it now. The hand gives up. Kenzo presses in like a button the nipple of the body that touched him. Kenzo is suddenly rolled over like a side of pork and the body tries to enter him anally. Then stops. The body shies away, rears up, is gone. Kenzo can almost hear his eyes blinking. Someone else comes down from the blaze of light. What happened before is repeated. And this time completed. It is cold, impersonal and frightening. His arse hurting like hell, Kenzo lies as still as an animal trying to blend in with its surroundings.

After some time, getting over his nervous exhaustion a little, he looks over to his left to see, of all things, a face smiling at him through the gloom. An arm, this time a friendly arm, extends through the darkness to touch Kenzo's hand. The face, so different from the other blurred granite faces, comes closer. It is that of a young person, foolish enough to be smiling aloud in a place like this. He and Kenzo embrace carefully, with some real feeling for they have liked the foolishness of the other. Both are two babes in the woods. They make a space in the night and dump their unusable stupidity and tenderness there. With reckless enthusiasm the boy drags his robe off and strips Kenzo of his. They then think they can make love. But no. They have provided the moment the creeping figures were waiting for. Kenzo and the boy have bared their flesh. In the figures crawl, stealthily and fixedly as jackals on the scent. Kenzo and the boy feel their meat being touched, pinched and squeezed. While they act out their love-making it has to become more and more of a simulation as the bloodless hands close in. Kenzo loses his erection but soon a thumb and forefinger have fixed vice-like at the base of his penis and they steadily work it as if trying to pull it up by the roots. The smile goes dead on the boy's face. Kenzo has learnt the secret of this place – you do your love-making under the quilts and never show an inch of your flesh. The nightmare suffocation of it all and the barely audible titters that could be heard when he protested that the hand was hurting him drive Kenzo out of the room to the toilet.

On returning, for he hasn't done with his curiosity yet, he finds the room quiet. Soon after lying down Kenzo finds the boy next to him again. They embrace and shelter under the cave of their thick quilt. They whisper their names and ages. The boy is nineteen. Hajime – from Kyoto, a student, his first time here too. Kenzo doesn't tell him he's a novice priest – Hajime'd probably think he'd be measured up for a funeral. Kenzo and Hajime murmur and touch each other under the safety of their quilt. Kenzo suddenly feels a giggle coming on. But swallows instead and puts his finger on Hajime's lips. Any orgasms are out of the question now though. A thousand bird-reptiles would descend out of the sky to feast on the flesh if any orgasm occurred. So Kenzo reaches back to the box of tissues at the head of the futon to blow his nose. Groping around for a moment he can't find his briefs. But here they are, tucked under the futon. He pulls them back into the cave.

The couple next to him have become naked and are in the positions of what is called love-making. Becoming spectators themselves, irresistibly, having never before beheld two humans performing sex, Kenzo and Hajime prop themselves up on their elbows to watch. Once again, like the sky being covered by clouds, the naked couple is blotted out by the gathering figures. When the shapes have had their fill, all rise together in a locust-swarm movement and take their prey with them. Vanished. All that is left is the turned-back quilt and the exposed bedding throbbing its whiteness fluorescently until it disappears into the gloom too.

Kenzo and Hajime hug more tightly together. The boy is afraid but tries not to show it. Kenzo is not afraid, just very tired and desirous of protecting Hajime. However, the closer Hajime nestles in and the more intent on sleeping undisturbed in Kenzo's arms he becomes the more restless to escape becomes Kenzo. He thrusts up. The boy is dragged up startled with him. They lurch out of the room. The hall light shows them each other's face. A pleasant but dubious surprise. Hajime is very beautiful. Too beautiful. Too sweet and open and vulnerable. Kenzo feels as if he has trodden on a soft anemone in the rock pools he was walking through barefoot. He feels an unfathomable desire to both hurt and caress Hajime with the same movement. (Whatever really did become of that Misa?, Kenzo suddenly again wants to know). Hajime and Kenzo try to speak even though they are rendered almost incapable of speech by their amazement at how their relationship is working backwards from touch to speech in reverse of how relationships usually proceed.

A group of men have gathered on the stairs to watch the blue movies being shown on the wall. Kenzo thinks this would be a good opportunity to escape. However, the projector and the reclining 40 | bodies determine to prevent him. He is incredulous at how a blue movie could foil his desire for freedom. He and Hajime have no choice but to return to the room. Lying there again, body to body, Hajime shrinking in closer with the every thresh of the rolling and groaning bodies now around them, Kenzo's heart is torn in two. He likes this boy and knows he must protect him but the fatal illusoriness and futility of it all – his desires, the boy's needs and the bodies grappling with one another, sicken him to the bottom of his heart. His curiosity has shut up like a clam shell. It wants to learn, see and feel nothing more. He must leave before it is too late. Hajime's sweet perspiration and unshaven chin must be driven away at all costs.

Kenzo leaves. Ploughs through the blue movie audience. Crashes the locker door as he gets back into his clothes as fast as possible before Hajime finds him. Kenzo must seal himself up without a crack showing, recover his composure and catch the last train home. But Hajime is sent by tormentors. Hajime, so transparent, white and hurtable himself, comes in and leans against his locker door and tries to smile at Kenzo. He is bewildered. Kenzo resolutely dresses. Squatting down to his bag, Hajime takes out a small subway map, tears it in half, writes his Kyoto address and phone number on it and pushes it into Kenzo's pocket. Kenzo, hating himself for his weakness, discovers himself giving Hajime his own phone number. In the face of that act he rushes out, as far away from bait as possible.

Ten minutes later he is sitting on a train, his arms folded, regarding the window opposite him and behind his cold fixed face shredding every memory of every experience he never had.

'What is it?' Linda felt something looking imploringly at her through the night. 'No, it's nothing. My mind's playing tricks.'

She'd been meditating, and her mind was finding it hard to settle into sleep now.

. . . A little tremor went through the room. Her eyes opened a moment. Then they closed, and she went to sleep.

4 It is one week later. The first Sunday of September. Though it's calendar autumn now it's still hot and humid. Kenzo has been working on his composition for piano, flute and drum every night of the week. But now a tide is going out and the moon is waning. Kenzo is depressed. He slowly turns the key in the lock of his dream room. He retreats inside. The world dissolves like a cloud into the sky.

And he thinks dully how he has had almost enough of unsatisfying sexual experiences, the heart of the experience always slipping out of grip just as you'd tightened your hand. (Experience as sacrifice – on a chac-mol.)

He is also depressed about his music. He feels that the mesh of his mind is too coarse to catch the gold specks filtering through him from the outside, that he cannot separate purely enough the sludge and ore of his existence. His music needs only the gold. He knows it is true indeed that beauty is potentially everywhere resting compact on the trigger which could so easily be set off, but right now he cannot see it. He is doubtful and anchored.

Ultimately though, after this mood has passed he knows that, given his energy and intent, he will not fail in his task of distilling what he knows of beauty into his music. Time is his only thwarter, time which evaporates as fast as it condenses. Kenzo feels acutely his urgency to complete the music before time runs out. Time frustrates him. His thrust always comes up against bone. He wants to destroy that which baulks him. He craves to break loose of his fetters. He must. He must leave himself as music. He is a human in a destructible body who yearns, as does everyone to a greater or lesser degree, to put a mark on something before all things vanish in time. No diamond exists that will be hard enough to resist him, he rails to himself. He shall tear the superflous away from his music, stripping existence down past its bones, refining the essence of it all into the music. And thus with such power he will rebuke all things.

But one second later Kenzo's mood collapses again and he

doesn't have any such power at all. The exhilarating intentions were all unfounded aggrandisements. Everything he does is false and weak. He is now vulnerable to the whole world and its doubts. The world outside his dream room reduces him in size and robs him of his weapons. In his weakness now he longs for Tatsuo and the security Tatsuo represents to protect him from the world. And from himself and his violent changes of mood.

It is only for the duration of his weakness however, that he requires the image of Tatsuo as reassurance. When he thinks hard enough about Tatsuo he asks himself if all that past faithfulness to him wasn't simply an excuse not to venture so very far into the non-temple world. Kenzo feels he cannot receive Tatsuo back with any open-heartedness until he's proved to himself he's no longer using Tatsuo as any excuse. And besides, now that Kenzo is feeling stronger, and he is becoming stronger again by the minute, the image of Tatsuo becomes an irritant since Kenzo's greater desire is to encircle and protect. He wants to grow out like the rings of a tree including deeply within himself all love, all weakness, all things and people. He will be that tree. He will let rest in his branches all things which crave harbour and rest. So he will eventually rock to peace sleep even himself.

Strong now, he sees it is the fluctuations of his moods themselves which thwart him, not time. From his dream room in his shadowed valley he stares for that somewhere x-point in the sky from which he could see his whole terrain as flat and moodless. That enviable point of paramount detachment and serenity. It can be reached only by the vehicle of his music.

The contemplation of that nearly impossible point tires him and in spite of himself he weakens again. He turns away and experiences the bitter exhaustion of knowing nothing he feels has any foundation. Yes there is power and beauty somewhere but somewhere is always a dust blown into the irretrievability of elsewhere.

Kenzo would now feebly stamp his foot in defiance in the little boat of himself which can so easily be capsized. He doesn't know who he is or what he is, or what it is that makes him do what he does. There is nothing but water, formless heavy water under and above him. Water and vapour and ever more water. His eyes are open only upon an infinite, pale and nebulous void. Nothing moves behind it or in it. He has no tangibility to cast shadows across that blankness. Neither can he cast shadows in the form of dreams. So what is he | 43 then, he wonders – the shadow itself of something he cannot see, sense or imagine? So what is he anyway? It no longer seems to matter.

Then there was a quiet, the quiet of the room or the spaces between the ticks of the metronome he used for his music. A quiet coming out of itself a roar inside out.

Grabbing his pillow he plugged his head up in the corner with it and screamed and screamed as if something trapped in his head were trying to split its way out as if glass were a thing which could simply tear apart.

Then everything stopped as suddenly as it had started. Like the end of the world. The quiet went back into him like a thing into its sheath and he fell along it onto his bed where he fell asleep so quickly he was already dreaming–

Dreaming of something he'd read in a magazine . . . Mercury sleet counterpoint glass swung money hollows in the palm sweaty twisting around and around a long loin cloth twisting a knot. Here, there. A knot. In the back, in the front. A youth is seen folding into the steam of a public bath by a weird Man seemingly harmless. Seen nearly every night of the week. But tonight the man is bold enough to ask the boy back to his home after the bath.

One day. Humid. Low obscure sky. Paper windows open. Bamboo green spikes. Shadows behind the thin paper. Shadows behind the sky, coming down, closer to the back of beauty. The youth comes in late. Cotton robe. Sweat band. Closer to the back of beauty. Man and boy squat on their heels on the wide tatami floor talking quietly, thin cups of green tea between them shivering porcelain under dragon and waterfall designs. Sipping heat.

Will the boy pose as model for the Man's camera? Will pay of course. Yes. For a magazine. Very professional like, you know . . . So then, just slip off your robe to see . . . Good. Good ox body young muscle planes pushing up fitted one under the other, streaks of sweat, proud shy smile, long twisted tight rope of cloth as loin cloth. Everything heavy and filled out. Short crew cut. Twisting turning up standing. Displaying. Hand over the breast hand on hip. Wider smile. Young and stupid. Flesh in the market, turning squatting down again. Clean white cloth holding the fat.

Is carefully observed.

44 | Well then we'll look at the garden. See what to do. Verandah

creaks under young and old flesh. Looking out. Wooden gibbet construction, platform underneath, pulley rope and chains.

Do you mind? Uh . . . Where's the camera?

Wrists bound between shoulder blades. Legs free to kick but much rope cutting into the trunk. Special rope up from the groin. Long rope out the back to lead the still smiling slave up onto the platform.

But where's the camera?

Never mind. Soon.

The rusty pulley hoists the load into the sky. Gravity forces the flesh down and the ropes go cruelly up . . . oooooooooooh pain beginning of course. Worse than he thought. The whole intention all along. The Man surveys it all. The peach swell in the loin cloth. Prodded with a handy bamboo pole as if it were fruit on a tree. Exquisite fallen mess, slippery underfoot. The skin coming off in the dream. The Dream. The dream at last the boy could be any boy multiplications of Hajimes and Tatsuos and Misas any and every youth full of semen and life and sperms and blood and life and the absolute verifications of existence going through existence to the other side of life where it is absolute and life and life yet again and life more and more every boy multiplying to slake your unending appetites going crazy bull horns in a wall. Stuck. Hard on sweating. The man tremblingly prods again and the sap in the tree retracts and groans and begs.

Now. Do you will you love me? I won't let you down until you do, the Man says. After a while the boy realises he's got no choice. Slowly, horribly, agonisingly, teeth biting his lips, he whispers, Yes, Yes I love you I will love you. But why oh why are you doing this to me?

It's the only way to make you love me. You see.

. . . Dangling heavier. Time passes. The proud head lolls saliva. Legs stop kicking midair. Nailed, caught. Then the rod quivers closer. But, but. God comes down and pushes the bully man over. What are you doing? Untie him. Stop it. You have to untie him yourself of your own free will. Even though I can you must do it. The man obeys.

When the boy is free again rubbing his red flesh God is satisfied and goes away, letting the man off lightly this time. But quietly slyly softly the man asks the boy if he'd do it all again. After some hesitation the boy says, Well . . . yes . . . probably Yes. The man | 45 says alright then let's do it again but don't scream or groan or God'll hear you. So let's go back to the public bath. . .

Uncontrollable shameful dreaming roaring waking Kenzo waking forcing himself to can't help twisting into the sheet bringing himself off as automatically savagely painfully as the upthrust of mattress flying open into groaning bitten back sheet in the mouth noiseless screaming downthrust of fist jagged into matter–

Five years ago at the temple Kenzo was woken at four-thirty am by the scurry of his brother's white-socked feet as he rang the bell along the corridor. Throwing on his robe Kenzo stumbled ahead to fall in line with his brown-robed brothers going silently in their rough straw sandals to their places in the meditation hall.

Passing his father the Roshi perched already upon his high wooden seat in the darkness Kenzo stood ready with the others at the round black cushions on the meditation ledges.

The priests bowed to the north, the south, the east and the west. They pressed their hands together in prayer. Swiftly and deftly they rose up onto the ledge, pushed their sandals beneath, settled on their cushions with legs crossed Lotus-style, made one turn to face the wall then swayed gently to the right and to the left to prepare their bodies for meditation.

The gong was struck. The bell rung thrice. The candle flames leaned in the wake of the priest with the stick. A rush of brown silk circumnavigated the room once quickly, then, slower and slower till the priest's feet fell with the measured regularity of a clock's beats. His shadow fell far ahead of him along the plaster wall. Sensing his approach Kenzo tucked his chin further in and made his back even straighter. For a moment he felt he couldn't breathe. Then he thought of everything in order to think of nothing. He succeeded to some extent. His blood stole through his body as softly and silently as the priest with the stick did through the hall. By the hesitant inch Kenzo eased himself into meditation and let the edges of his mind dissolve. He tried to become his favourite image – a fly seized in amber.

About a half an hour later, from the temple, issued a steady and regular sound. One of the priests was striking the drum to signal the beginning of the end of the meditation. A bell was then struck. Birds could be heard outside. The air shivered under the impacts of the gong. Those moments in their beauty deeply impressed Kenzo's then stilled and quieted mind.

As the blood slowly began to circulate again in his numb legs his mind fetched itself back from where it had gone. The priests all stirred. They exhaled almost all together. They swayed again to the right and to the left. Kenzo's father shifted in his wooden throne. The priest with the stick blew out the candles.

The priests were then permitted to file out and go to their sleeping room to roll up and put away their bedding, throw open the shutters and run on all fours along the floorboards, backsides in the air, with soft rags polishing the wood smoother than dark shell.

At the summons of another bell they then scuttled off to breakfast in the low wide room overlooking the garden. The sun had fully risen. The tree tops moved in the breeze. Holding their bowls up at chin level the priests filed into the room. Sitting on their heels they unwrapped their bowls and set them to the right and to the left in accordance with the ritual. Kenzo's father's eyes were those of a conductor as they seemed to guide everyone's fingers around and under their bowls and utensils. He sat with stern mildness at his own little table at the head of the long ones. Kenzo's attention was perhaps more diverted by the expression on his father's face than it was supposed to be. The simple and beautiful designs on Kenzo's lacquered bowls also used to hold his attention and nearly delay him in holding out his bowl to be filled with steaming rice out of the wooden bucket. Two of the priests hauled those buckets up and down the room, each of the other priests accepting the portions of food which were dished out. Sometimes it was Kenzo's turn to carry the buckets but really he preferred sitting and eating inconspicuously to the business of the allocation of food.

The soup and pickles and tofu prepared by Kenzo's mother in the adjoining kitchen were handed along next, their journey interrupted by the regulated bows of the priests' heads and the pressings-together of their hands as they paid respect for being able to receive and pass on plates of food.

Then with a sharp crack of his wooden clappers Kenzo's father the Roshi signalled that the eating could begin. One eye had to be kept on how fast the Roshi ate for as soon as he finished, by tradition, everyone else had to finish. Unfortunately he usually took less food than Kenzo did so Kenzo was hard pressed to have his breakfast gobbled down before his father laid down his sticks neatly across his bowl.

Not a word was ever spoken. All communication, if any, was done by stylised gestures and glances. All noise was forbidden. Kenzo knew too well how his father's eyes would freeze if Kenzo was hapless enough to drop a chopstick or accidentally let his bowls knock together. And all offensive sights such as even the emptying of the bit of rinsing water back into the refuse bucket had to be concealed with a polite inclination of the hand.

On finishing the meal the priests cleaned their bowls where they sat. Here the height of the ceremony was reached. Thin slices of pickled yellow radish were swiftly passed along for wiping the bowls clean. Then there was the complicated but ingrained method of wrapping the bowls together again in their cloths, with a small knot here and a deft tuck there. All these movements were rigorously controlled, pared down to an absolute minimum of motion, mechanicalised in order that the priests' minds be left free of distraction so that they could accept the enlightenment which they were perpetually and relentlessly told could strike down like lightning at any moment.

Breakfast done, the priests went after a short break to the main temple hall for the first Sutra chanting of the day. That Kenzo loved but took care not to display to the others an over-enthusiasm for drums, chanting and gongs. Enthusiasms for anything save enlightenment were firmly discouraged.

Facing the Buddha altar the priests dropped to their knees, pressed the floor with their foreheads, got up, fell to the floor again and repeated the whole process thrice. The Roshi, purple silk sash now thrown over his shoulder, rose and fell as nimbly as the youngest of the novice priests. As Kenzo watched his father and moved in synchronism with him, Kenzo was convinced he thought he knew where this path of his was to lead. He thought that enlightenment lay within attainability even though the mountains and rivers of the spirit had to be crossed for him to get there. All arrows seemed to point in the one direction but where that pointed-to-place exactly was Kenzo didn't know. He went about the spartanly pious and devout routine because that was what he had led himself and been led to believe was best. He strove so hard he found himself going one step forward two steps backwards even though any sage priest on being asked would have told him that desperately trying too hard to reach enlightenment was the best way not to get it. Enlightenment really just falls on one like a piece of sky or meteor, anywhere, at any time. But Kenzo mistakenly thought it was all just a matter of energy and will power. He butted at what he thought had to be the door to enlightenment but which was not a door and never had been and never would be for enlightenment knows no 'doors'.

For the time being however, there in the temple, listening to his father lead the droning of the beautiful Sutras, Kenzo let himself be persuaded by the chants and the gong that maybe the supposedly somewhere door to enlightenment lay through those musical things. So he listened more carefully. His voice rose and fell in unison with the others. What they chanted – the Pali, the Sanskrit, the Chinese and the Japanese words all strung together to make a kind of Buddhist Esperanto, he often couldn't understand. But the words didn't matter. It was the beat of the music that carried him effortlessly along towards at least some kind of peace. His younger brother, producing the thick and definite sounds on the drum by the altar, seemed to become blissfully inseparable from the instrument. Object and subject, forever separate, forever combined – at least Kenzo thought he could grasp that Law of the fundamental union of all things no matter how superficially divided they always seemed to be. The drum, the music; his father, his mother; the tree, the bird; the All the One – Kenzo could have cheerfully marched out of the temple there and then with that bit of knowlege in his head and never have been the poorer for it. But he plodded on, suspicious that the All the One was not enough. And he was informed by his father that it was indeed not enough: it should have been the All the One, the both and neither, everything and nothing and then yet again the All the One. In principle, that is. The application of it to what Kenzo could feel, see and smell remained to be tested.

The Roshi droned on. The priests rose and fell thrice again to bring the ceremony to an end. Passing the Buddha image the priests pressed their hands together and bowed their heads. Then they went to the gardens and fields to hoe, weed and plant. Nearly everything the priests ate came from their own gardens so it was a great joy for Kenzo to be able to tend and cultivate those plants. Then after washing their feet and picking the dirt out from under their fingernails they herded again to the meditation hall for the late morning sitting. The late morning meditation was always the most difficult for Kenzo, having just come back in from the fresh air diffusing and relaxing his concentration. Often did he then receive a blow on the shoulder from his brother's waddy for not sitting up straight enough. Kenzo was consequently more pleased to leave the hall at the end of the meditation than he had been to enter it.

Lunch was the pivot of the day. From then on the second half of the day, with near perfect symmetry, repeated backwards the first half. The closer nightfall approached the more elated or depressed Kenzo tended to become, much to the horror of his father. Kenzo didn't know why he felt like that. He knew it was not good to be prone to extremes of mood as they are inclined to upset the peaceful equilibrium which is all-important in any temple. But Kenzo was nonetheless irresistibly swept away by storms and breezes to horizons miles away from where he was supposed to be going. And as time went by it happened more often. His family was relieved when it came time for Kenzo to enter the Daikuma Buddhist university in Tokyo to begin the academic training necessary for a novice priest.

But it soon became apparent to Kenzo, after a year had passed at the university, that the academic way wasn't going to be any solution to anything, either.

' . . . So Linda,' says Kenzo, folding his arms, 'after all I've said about daily life in the temple have I put you off yet? Are you still interested in becoming a nun one day? You might have more success with Zen than I've had . . . ' He thinks for a moment. He has to talk to someone, and there's no one better than Linda. '. . . As you know, I'm the oldest son in my family. I'm expected to assume leadership of my father's temple one day, and that means I'll have to marry and have the sons who'll take over after me – It's all still like a sixteenth-century craft guild – In other words I should expect myself to put my homosexuality, for just one little thing, down to some earthly illusion I've postponed meditating away, get married and be a round peg in a round hole. I can't do it.'

Linda stirs in her seat. She has been so closely following what Kenzo was telling her about the temple and is so impressed and disquieted by how he told his story, she doesn't say anything yet. She lights another cigarette and finishes off the remains of her coffee. 'But,' she begins after a moment, 'can't you just tell your father you don't want to be a priest and drop the Buddhist studies and let one of your younger brothers be groomed for the leadership role?'

Kenzo laughs, 'I'd have to die first before a younger brother could step in – Their lives are already set on their own courses.

Everything's so fixed and decided at the temple. It's like a machine – pull out one part and the whole lot breaks down. Zen is like a machine set in motion centuries ago and the meditation ledges are conveyor belts turning out identical enlightened ornaments which are then sat on shelves for the rest of their lives . . . No, I'm sorry. I'm exaggerating. But what you say has a point – The problem is though, I'd be perfectly happy to be a devout Buddhist, if I didn't have to do it in the way already prescribed for me; and the way in which I don't like what I've merely inherited would not be, to the people I've inherited it from, an acceptable reason for abandoning what I've inherited. My objections and contrary desires would be seen as just so many manifestations of Maya-illusion, which would just need a thorough meditation for them to be gotten rid of. You know, the whole thing's so involved and contradictory I can't even begin to think my way out of it – most people in my position solve the problem of the clashes between the spiritual way of life and their inherited environments and the ways by which they want to live by various shades of grey compromises. But I . . .'

But I what? he wants to know of himself, looking down at the table. While talking he's also been considering to himself where his defiant little sexual revolution of late has been getting him. He now feels a foolish latecomer to the sexual revolution begun in the sixties and now ending it seems, thanks to the new puritanical morality pulpitting its way out of America, where the in-tandem of the puritanism – the upsurge of the virulent sexually-transmitted diseases such as AIDS, herpes, and hepatitis B and so on and hell only knows what, also got its melting-pot boost. All those people out there reaping the whirlwind of what they have sown and here's me little Kenzo still so close to his old Buddhist morality he wouldn't be able to tell which was hot on the heels of which – his old morality or the any new morality public or private sexual revolutions are supposed to bring about.

Then he sees it all in something of a flash – I, Linda and Harriet are fundamentally in a bind – I have the dilemma of a religion I never chose to receive; Linda and Harriet see Buddhism as some salvation-route they've chosen, having, as they have, turned their backs on their inherited Christian backgrounds. But that Buddhism of theirs, is just a long or short passing phase for Linda, and Harriet too. They will discover, if they haven't done so already, that traditional mainstream Buddhism is just as inefficient an old $\quad$ | 51 passenger liner for crossing the seas as is traditional Christianity. Both splinter on the reefs of the twentieth century into all those countless fragment cults now, including the fundamentalist cults which claim to be the original whole and not the broken parts they really are . . . He thinks. So is this really true? he asks himself; if it's true it would be unbearably inconvenient to the need to live in hope for answers and solutions.

Kenzo has been trained to disbelieve everything he 'thinks', for according to Zen 'thinking' itself is disbelief, illusion, the shadow of the object, so when he now puts such vain 'thinking' out of his mind his Buddhist training has actually done him the backhand service of causing him to dismiss the disbelief it encourages, in the same moment as it dismisses the doubts about itself which could threaten its survival in the mind which would disbelieve too much.

After the waiter gives them their second coffees, Linda, mindful that Kenzo never finished what he was going to say before, but not wanting to draw him back to it, says, '. . . You said you were involving yourself in that music . . . One thing I can't quite understand is how you should so suddenly have started writing music. Do you use notes and stuff? I didn't know you had any musical experience.'

'Nor did I.' Kenzo smiles. 'But all of a sudden I did . . . start writing something, one day, after Tatsuo went away. Maybe writing music's enlightenment,' he laughs. 'But sometimes I think I'm writing it because of Tatsuo. He writes music. Maybe I want to get closer to him by doing something he does. Or, maybe even the music is for him, to him . . . I'm not sure.'

'You're very fond of him?'

'Something like that . .' Kenzo goes on to talk about his music.

His fingers handling the cigarette are pale and fine-boned – we both smoke too much, Linda thinks, against the better judgement of public censure. Kenzo once didn't smoke so much. Linda remembers – the lunch in the grass, the swoop of the temple roof above the green hill. Kenzo in his robes, standing there, smilingly examining the wedge of tomato between his chopsticks. Harriet having a snooze under her cloth hat.

She feels again now how much she likes his face. He has large, clear eyes, with an expression of ironic softness. His lips are well defined and firm. Linda feels a desire to put her own lips on his. She doesn't think it is a sexual feeling. Kissing him, she feels, would be more an act of verifying a bond than it would be any testing out of anything sexual.

Hoping he'll go on talking so as to leave her to quietly enjoy looking at him, (and also to pleasantly wonder at the little Buddhist effigy he gave her today as a present) she feels that whatever Kenzo might say would be somehow important to her. She wonders if he is aware that she has never met anyone quite like him before. A little embarrassed by the strength of her feeling for him, Linda looks down into her cup and picks it up to take a sip quite unaware that while Kenzo has been talking he's been regarding her in a rather similar way. Something about Linda is attractive to him. Whether it's her openness, her bursts of vivacity or what radiates from her clear blue eyes he doesn't know, and doesn't really want to find out, being quite satisfied as he is with being with her and enjoying that feeling that only she, out of all the people he has ever known, creates in him. She relaxes him, thaws him out. Sitting with her in this coffee shop is a restful detour the end of which, proclaimed by his watch, fills him with a feeling of dread. Once he says goodbye to her he'll be again at the mercy of himself. To him, Linda's eyes flash, in their blueness, like the sky itself, that open sky which he feels is disappearing from him.

Despite his Zen stoicism, he now feels tempted to say something which might win her sympathy further.

She seems to sense this, and says, '. . . Finish your studies. . . Even if your heart's not really in it you should still continue. Don't leave things unfinished. . .'

'I understand what you mean . .' The waiter has come up to ask them if they'd like anything else. Kenzo and Linda order tea. As the young waiter leans over the table to clear away the coffee cups Kenzo can see diagonally down through the boy's open shirt to a nipple slanting away on the smooth brown swell where a faint red mark can also be seen.

Kenzo feels a quarrel within himself – Tatsuo seemed to think that just because he came from a temple he had to be 'good'. That illusion of people such as Tatsuo makes him feel lonely, disobedient, and contemptuous. Perversely, it takes all your Zen training to be sensible about such negativities. And nothing is more expected of a priest than to be 'sensible'. That smooth brown swell makes him feel cold, with apprehension. You can never have another body, completely.

The waiter moves away, and with him some release of Kenzo's conviction he is going wholly insane, an insanity which encompasses the Maya-illusion it is and the any meditation which would deny the insanity.

Yet a different, perhaps unflinching part of his mind can resume what he was going to say to Linda as if the thoughts just then had never existed, as if they bore no relation whatsoever to what he now says: 'One thing I'm worried about is that I don't think I can stand alone . . . I need crutches . . . I had Zen as a crutch even though that, according to Zen, is the last thing you should regard as a crutch; in fact, ultimately, to be really enlightened, you have to one day give up even Zen itself – swim the river alone naked. But I made a crutch of it. Now the music is a crutch. If that fails too I don't know what I'll fall back on. After that, there seems to be nothing. I cannot use myself – any quintessence of self, as a crutch because I still believe the Buddhist idea that there is no such thing as individual essences or even "individuality" at all for that matter. After the illusion of having an individual soul is destroyed there is nothing left at all. No crutches. Nothing . . . ' Kenzo suddenly feels he is about to grasp the truth of what has been troubling him recently, but no sooner has he felt that than it slips out of grasp again.

Linda is uneasy at hearing what Kenzo said since she herself has looked upon Zen as some escape route of herself, a crutch of sorts. She feels the need now to say with forced cheer, 'Don't look at things that way. Take it easy about your future, I wouldn't worry about it. It'll look after itself. You don't have to make a masterpiece of your music . . .' She stops. Linda has a certain switch-off point when anything about her threatens to consume her. Her cheerfulness comes down like a curtain before the act has finished. Her lightness, which relaxes more single-minded people and attracts them to her, is exactly what so effectively distracts her from seeing anything through to its conclusion. She is a glider floating on any wind, a flower never sinking in any water. It is fortunate for her that Kenzo, who would go as a stone through anything he might hit, is not aimed at her.

'Alright then,' he says, smiling, 'I won't worry about anything.' They are both silent for a while.

54 | They drink their tea, and watch the water falling in the ornamental

fountain in the middle of the coffee shop . . . Linda says, lighting a cigarette, 'I don't know but, most people, when they're about twenty, wonder why they're living, forget about it, and then just start surviving. Once people have gotten through a few early disappointments and crises they can get through the rest of life fairly well by just hanging on tight and not asking too many questions. Survival. Whatever threatens survival is thrown overboard as ballast. No matter how miserable their lives may be people hang onto them. Just living from day to day, only surviving – It's not enough for me . . . What do you think is an important thing to live by?'

'To keep your vision. If you've got one.'

'What do you mean by "A vision"?'

'I'm not sure. It's just a feeling. It's not poetic or spiritual. It's both of them and yet neither of them. It's just something. When you become aware you've got it you start nurturing it and letting it grow, you keep it inside you, and when it grows stronger, if it's not killed by bitterness or disillusionment, it starts nurturing you and you are eventually enclosed within it and you see the world through it. It protects you from the world and yet it allows you to move through the world more easily than if you didn't have it.'

'So it's an egg within you until you become an egg within it – eternally hatching?' She cannot resist making a little joke of Kenzo's seriousness. But she's glad he's talking about visions now and not about the troubles of coping with Buddhism. She prefers him to be her mentor, an illuminator, and not any agitator of spiritual discontent.

'I suppose so,' Kenzo says.

'How do you know if you've got it?'

'If you've got it you definitely know it – The world looks different. I'm not saying you see the world "for what it really is" or anything like that because the world can be anything at all, there being so many worlds as there are people to perceive them. You just see things differently, sideways somehow, or a little from the back. Not like the sun. The sun looks the same from any angle but not this world – It is like a cloud with ever-changing recesses and angles. Have you ever seen a cloud just dissolve into the sky and then in another place just seem to form again? This world, like a cloud, depends on the sun's light for it to be seen. If there is no light there is no world . . . ,' Kenzo trails off, his words evaporating away.

Linda feels a little dubious about such poetry, though having been | 55 at first interested. She feels the need to get him back to what she asked originally. 'But what really is the most important thing you try to live by? It sounds like something connected to an interpretation of what beauty is.'

'. . . Yes. It is something beautiful. Like a cloud, beauty has recesses and angles. There is an exact position a certain distance away from beauty from which it must be observed. Like a good painting. It is incoherent if it is seen too close up or from too far away – Too close you just see pigment grains, too far away it's a blur. An ashtray seen close up is a glass wall and from too far away it is only a shape without an obvious purpose. You have to learn the exact position from which to see beauty properly.'

'Do you?'

'Yes. Maybe beauty is like a dream. It has no awareness of any other reality except itself. A feature of dreams is that while being experienced they are rarely aware of other states, compared with the dim but sure awareness we have in wakefulness of having dreamed a dream. A dream, in its paradoxical way, though contingent for existence upon everything but itself, is totally self-sufficient. A dream is free to go in any or all directions. It is also free to dream within itself of itself.'

'You really think so? You still haven't answered my question.'

'That? I said I think I live by a vision.'

Linda suddenly understands how Harriet must often feel with her – impatient with vagueness. She opens her mouth to say something to pin him down, but she gives up. She feels an exalted form of greed to hear more of what Kenzo's 'Vision' really is, but since he is evading her she feels she had better stop persisting. She has a suspicion Kenzo may have been playing one of his obscure teasing Zen tricks on her.

Whether or not Kenzo was mildly teasing Linda with his clouds and dreams cannot be judged from his face now. He is looking anxiously vacant, his arm on the table where he can see the time clearly on his watch. Linda will be soon putting her cigarettes and lighter back into her bag, to get ready to go and teach at five o'clock.

They said goodbye near Shinjuku station. Kenzo then turned to walk
down one of the vast stairways into the echoing and booming station.
The peak hour now was a great long steady wind funnelling down
into the station as if the world were a hole in space through which not
enough could ever pass.

5

Kenzo moved with the crowd along the underground way.

A youth was approaching from the opposite direction. Kenzo's
eyes sharpened. The youth and Kenzo soon passed, and Kenzo felt
desire. A sudden, overpowering desire. He started to feel that
tightness across the head. The roaring of blood behind the eardrums.
Couldn't hear himself as he saw in everywhere dove-tailing mirrors
his hands press in around the youth's neck.

The boy far away now, Kenzo dropped out of the crowd and
leaned up against a pillar. Some perspiration. A sensation of illness.
The sparkling grits in the concrete staring at him.

That which I can never get.

He was now clinically insane with.

Linda moves about her apartment as if in a hurry, getting the
groceries into the fridge and the vegetables out of their bags. She's
bothered about Kenzo. When they were walking from the coffee
shop this afternoon he seemed particularly restless and troubled.
She wishes they could've talked longer to get to the bottom of things.
She is convinced, as always, that he is good, striving for some
sincere, tested, greater goodness, but she is sure there's something
in him he's trying to fight, a darkness which she doesn't know where
to begin to understand.

She must meditate, forget her forebodings and clear her mind.
She must meditate.

She draws the curtains and locks the door. She gets out her black velvet cushion which Kenzo's mother made for her, sets it down in the corner of the room, settles herself on it, legs in the Lotus position, then makes her spine as straight as possible, tucks in her chin and sways to the right and to the left in preparation for her daily meditation.

As soon as her breathing becomes light and regular and her mind rested (superficially though, a skin forming over the milk) the initial chaos begins being stirred up as if by a turbine. She is ready for that. The initial chaos of contemplation is a necessary prelude to any real advancement into proper meditation.

And so it begins.

She sees a gold Buddha statue as large as a star suspended in space. This image, she sees, or rather, pictures, almost every night. Then the Buddha has a moustache painted on his face. Then the Buddha becomes the Virgin Mother in Michelangelo's *Pietà* cradling the dead Christ. The Buddha star then increases in size until it blots out everything, becomes a blank screen upon which more images appear.

Linda sees a pig run up a tree, a tree among thousands on a cliff above a vast valley rich with autumn colours. The pig gives birth to another pig in the tree, then eats it. The pig throws itself over the cliff, falls, but never reaches the bottom of the chasm. It vanishes to be replaced by a purple leaf falling upwards which eventually comes to rest as a gilded leaf in a crown.

Then she sees a flayed man whose legs are being nibbled at by crabs. A long stool curves up between his legs as he cries out and gives birth to a baby girl from the heel of his foot. A set of silver and glass revolving doors turn. Men and women in evening dress dine off quail and lamb by candlelight in a space station slowly circling Mars. The universe emerges at the end of an eye dropper. Linda eats a leaf. Pigs and cows trample up the stairs of a tower to rooms where maidens are sleeping swathed in their long golden hair. The Buddha takes Christ down from the Cross. Down a green hill runs Kenzo clutching his brown robes. The pigs and cows butt in the doors and the screaming maidens dash their heads against the wall rather than be done to death by the animals. The universe, disguised as the universe, passes through the glittering revolving doors. Men and women set down their knives and forks and listen. Space creaks. The dish runs away with the spoon and the little dog laughs and Kenzo is going to be flown into. Now with a shove in the back each from the Buddha beautiful youths and maidens with rings on their fingers swing down by the million on long silver ropes through the universe. The mountains have never risen more sharply and the skies have never been more sapphire. The air is ringingly clear. A book swings open and all the letters fall out. Linda files her life in an empty space in the circular library where universes are as small as full stops on the ends of sentences. She falls through the bookcase. Alice in Wonderland beckons her from the other side of the mirror. But Linda can't fit through. The Nickies tear her away. The air separates for an instant and a chant can be heard as a demon pursues an angel. Linda sees it all. The angel then hid in Kenzo but when the danger passed it discovered it couldn't get out again. That evening the three of us went to the disco. The angel's been struggling to get out of Kenzo ever since. He doesn't know it. Through a rapidly contracting hole in the air she catches a blurred glimpse of the outcome. And that the angel will come back. To her. The little dog laughs and the pig runs away with the secret. Linda calls out to Kenzo who can't hear her because of the songs of a million silver creatures swinging across the universe. They fly overhead. The Buddha croaks like a giant frog. He wipes off his moustache. Men and woman take up their knives and forks again. A car roars past the room. The images then spin so fast they blur black, then grey, then white then are transparent. Linda can see right through. Her spine has never been straighter and her breathing never steadier. She is forgetting backwards. The hurricane rises and rises into the sky until it is a dot disappearing. Another car roars past her room. Her mind is forcing her to be disturbed by external sounds so that she can come out of her meditation for her own safety. Now wide-eyed staring at the wall Linda tries to repeat aloud what she has seen. But she can't because she doesn't believe it – Sheer fanciful madness. Undisciplined meditation.

She gets up, turns off the light, goes to bed, and dreams nothing.

And dreamed everything. He was told. A bit of wet dream flaking off the sheet Tatsuo curls up stomach muscles his navel disappearing morning. He was told to leave in his dream. He's not going to cancel the telegram this time and keep Linda and Kenzo waiting. The mark of the sun across the bed it's unbearable once too often millions of cells falling away from the nakedness first thing in the morning he grabs the telephone before it's too late before the mirror over there wakes up. Can't change his mind now he breathes into the receiver Hello cable office I'm coming back to Tokyo. Put that.

Sea and sky waiting for him outside the sun is ready for the last time now reflecting in the mirror on his heel catching up with a day too far away from his birth.

He turns on his heel away from the piano. The music is finished. It is done, finished. A friend of Tatsuo's from the college copied down this morning what Kenzo played to him. Piano then flute then drum. It's done and Kenzo doesn't care if the friend transcribed correctly or not. He is empty now. A gun has been fired. He awaits the avalanche's falling. Nothing but instincts remain within him. Time, once wastable, has eked away to a dripping.

He turns again and faces the piano. The making of the music depended upon a coil coiling tighter and tighter within him. It cannot decrease in size any further. A solid lump of tension now, an imploded lump, the only release is outwards. The music rose the music fell. Swirling, swelling, ever swirling upwards, then falling just before it might've burst through the glass dome over it to the point in the sky from where everything can be seen. The architecture of it is to forever contain it. The way for it to go through the glass without breaking it he has yet to discover.

A bee without its sting now there is little left for Kenzo to do except scribble a note for Tatsuo who is supposed to be returning sometime today to tell Tatsuo to meet him in Kamakura at ten tomorrow so that they can perhaps enjoy the beach and some swimming. That done, Kenzo considers the letter he's written Linda. He deconsiders it, and crumples it up and throws it into his desk drawer. There are other papers about too – blank enrolment forms for the autumn semester at Daikuma uni. The enrolments were today. Kenzo didn't show up.

Then he rummages about in the junk on the desk top for some money little left for he's given it nearly all away . . . It is Saturday night – The instinct is upon him. He itches to go out. He must go out as there is now nothing else to do. Into his bag he quickly packs a toothbrush, a beach towel, an apple and a fruit knife.

Linda is lying on her bed in the darkness. She is staring at the ceiling. A coldness is creeping up her spine. A shudder of inexplicable fear goes through her.

Kenzo enters the disco. Few people there. Without giving the usual swift glance around he hoists himself up on a bar stool and orders a rum and coke. In the mirror behind the bar he can see the dance floor without having to turn around. There dancing is a foreigner with the high bald face of a Flemish portrait, jiggling as if a giant marionette with a poppet Japanese boy frisking about like a lamb on stiff pointed feet.

Kenzo is seized with a desire to dance. In an instant he turns and asks the person sitting next to him to dance. The boy sighs with relief (he's been sitting waiting here since the place opened) smiles, and they go onto the dance floor and dance as if possessed. The boy – Kuni – is dressed in a suit with a bright red tie. Only eighteen years old he works in the City Hall of his home town and has just come to Tokyo by himself for the weekend. He can't stop smiling and talking. He is as fresh as a newly sharpened pencil. His teeth become ultra-violet in the changing lights. Kenzo likes him and almost forgets what has taken place today and how he felt before entering the disco. The vitality and joy with which they dance is something from many weeks ago for Kenzo. Kuni dances closer. Kenzo feels his blood flex and tingle. He knows what's stretching within him cannot go much further but he continues dancing and aggravating the course along which he is headlong flying.

An hour later Nicky is to be seen in the crowd with a tooth over the rim of his beer glass. The whites of his eyes sweep the dance floor like searchlights. He is unavoidable. Kenzo must go over to him and have his ear bashed with the dramatic story of Nicky's being fitted out with bridgework. The crocodile jaws open on a cracked and smoky laugh. Nicky's attention becomes fixed on Kuni who has now sidled up. The muscle in Kuni's arm is squeezed by Nicky followed up by a wink. Kenzo moves Kuni off towards the door. Nicky jeers after them and hoots with laughter.

In the taxi Kuni tells his life story to Kenzo. Feeling soothed, Kenzo thinks about what he likes in such youths – their irrepressible desire to confess and with touching stupidity lay all their cards on the table before one and all. A short but eventful life so far. Kuni has had about nine lovers. The most recent an American painter who lived in Paris for two years before coming to Japan to prepare a one-man exhibition. Kuni darkly and softly speaks of his hurt at that fifty-year-old's doing. Kuni turns his eyes to Kenzo expecting he's been looking out of the window. But no. Kenzo's eyes have been fixed on the side of Kuni's face all along.

Kuni takes charge. Kenzo passively lets Kuni direct the taxi driver to a new luxury hotel Kuni knows. It seems to Kenzo that there was no way his life could have avoided eventuating in this, in the stoppings and turnings of this taxi. But that's all he feels. Kuni begins paying for everything. The taxi driver first then an unnecessary tip for the porter in the hotel lobby. He is a proud working man and opportunities for treating others are so few, his being so young. The staff behind the counter with smooth celerity and arrogant obsequiousness issue Kuni with keys and breakfast cards. The smile Kenzo thought he saw playing on the corners of the lips of the receptionist makes him feel so old and jaded as he crosses the intolerably wide carpet desert to the elevator. Kuni is already inside pushing buttons and pretending to be an elevator boy. Then they become tense as they near their room. Kuni's youthfulness suddenly makes Kenzo feel as if this was the very first time he'd ever gone to a hotel with anyone. And yet, despite the fact he is only twenty-four, he feels so old.

Inside the room, Kuni throws his bags aside and lies down on the bed pretending to sleep. Kenzo laughs. Then has a shower. The havoc of the cold then hot water realerts him to his body and what will be expected of it soon. Each second of washing, drying and cleaning his teeth seems pitched to the last point of inevitability. He recalls his meditations under the leaning candle flames and tries without success to think of nothing. His tightening skin reflects the mirror as he passes it.

On returning to the bedroom every detail there jumps out in silhouette. Kuni, now in yukata and solemnly wearing spectacles watching the coin-TV, has pulled the two single beds together. Kenzo lies down on his half. A watch ticks against the pain in his head. Bedlamp glow. Kuni lurches around the room refolding clothes which have already been folded to death. He suddenly dives under the sheet and shuts his eyes tight. Kenzo smiles. He extends an arm and begins what has to be begun. Everything is too nervous at first. A long time is spent achieving nothing. Kuni goes naked to the toilet to noisily empty his bladder. When he comes back into the room Kenzo tells him to stand there with the bathroom light behind him – Underarm. Pectoral curve. Aside cock. Kenzo can be aroused by that. Kuni makes a flying belly flop back into bed and threshes around trying to expend some energy. He chides Kenzo for being too soft and gentle. Kuni wants roughness. He makes Kenzo bind his wrists and ankles with their gown cords. Now he arches and stretches, health and sinews, a clear bud appearing at the top of his erection. Kenzo, like the instrument he is becoming, obliges Kuni with his lowering lips. A salty cloud throbbing in his mouth. Kuni makes an affected cry of orgasm delight. Kenzo is shrinking, a coil tightening, the world flaking off the world, the every sight and sound blurring as if on a worn tape. The voices become slower. He cannot protect Kuni and Kuni cannot protect him. The crown of the tree sways leafless and restless.

Kenzo gets his apple and knife. Kuni giggles under the pleasure of having the cold apple rolled heavily across his belly and squirms under the thrill of the blunt side of the knife pressing in between his balls. He loves being tied up. Kenzo hates his being tied up. Kenzo unpicks the knots and throws the cords aside. Kuni is now too drowsy to groan aloud with disappointment and lets Kenzo diligently mop up the stray semen which is rapidly losing its whiteness. Then Kuni expects to be able to fall asleep in Kenzo's arms. He will do so. Staring at the pale eyelids closed before him Kenzo watches a sky for the bird he now knows will descend to be harboured by the tree. Where you can't hear yearning agony loneliness. A scream in ice you can't hear. A baboon-human static noiseless shrieking behind blurred red bars. A reaching forward. In the instant the glass finally stretched Kuni's left breast became under where a sliver of the explosion penetrated with Kenzo throwing himself over Kuni to protect him from any more. Kuni's eyes flashed wordless open at staring far walls opening on a horizon he'd never seen before his hands gripping into Kenzo's hair. Mouth opening and opened again. But no sound came out.

Silhouettes flying from the door to the bed pectoral armpit sweat redness wetness Kenzo felt his hair being gradually released. Saw the eyes close before him. Withdrew the knife and let it slide off the bed. He drew Kuni calmly into his arms and brought their bodies together. Only blood separated their nakedness. He lay silently like that with Kuni and his breathing became steadier and steadier. And there was no enormity no surprise. Nothing anymore.

At two the next morning Kenzo crossed the hotel lobby and got into a taxi. After he had the taxi stop at a corner in Shinjuku he walked the streets made out of nothing until the trains began running at five am. He caught a train to Kamakura. He sat on the beach until ten when Tatsuo arrived.

How funny to see Tatsuo after all this time, he thought. They drank beer. Tatsuo told him he hadn't changed a bit. They drank more beer and became a little drunk. And dared a public kiss.

Off the end of a pier Tatsuo swam. Kenzo lay against fishing baskets and watched. Shut his eyes against the sun. The sound of the pier creaking and Tatsuo's diving into the water. The cobalt and veridian water split and shivered and came back together over Tatsuo's heels. He flickered to the surface laughing. Twisted. His hand grabbing the water for support. Shouted cramped. Kenzo stood up. Dived in without a moment's hesitation.

He managed to pull Tatsuo a couple of metres or so but then Tatsuo's twisting weight and his inability to swim far proved too much. In a last effort to keep Tatsuo afloat he doubled under him to support him. The water twisted, his lungs ballooning. When the nearby boat reached them Tatsuo was feebly treading water trying to roll the now-drowned Kenzo over.

Soon a crowd started to gather on the beach under the brilliant blue sky.

The sun fell onto the sea.

Part
Two

To the west, on this clear November afternoon, the limits of Tokyo can be seen, disappearing where the mountain ranges, carved with snow, rise mauve under where the sun is gradually setting. The snow-capped peaks and deep ravines can be clearly seen, but not where the concrete and steel of Tokyo actually peter out at the foothills. The city, rippled as ocean beneath the wide windows of the tall Sumitomo building, laps as eddy at the foothills of the mountains. Looking out from the window is like peering from a lighthouse at the distant mainland beyond. And there the sun, becoming larger and redder, is setting. It will set behind Mt Fuji's shoulder. A sharp but graceful shoulder. If the eye stays long enough upon the mountains the barely perceptible colour changes of the peaks can be seen. Today, being windy and smogless after last night's rain, has been clear enough for the subtle atmospheric changes to be observed. On the observation floor of the skyscraper, people are mounting their cameras on tripods in preparation for the magnificent sunset that will surely take place soon. Other people, content with their eyes and memories, are just pressing against the windows to watch. The sunset is still a few minutes away yet.

Harriet, after a shriek at seeing a table vacant by the window, grabs Linda and gets them firmly installed at that table. The waiter's tray of cheesecakes was nearly sent twirling by the rapid passage of Harriet's elbows through the air. Then, heedless of the waiter's scornful look, Harriet gets herself out of her coats and into the menu as quickly as she can.

Linda waits for Harriet to let her see the menu. Today, Harriet's usual outburst of hair has assumed a tight orangeish shape, with a peeling of hair hanging down the side. It looks painfully tight at the hairline.

The strong sun coming in through the window makes Linda frown a little. Harriet, on looking up, interprets the frown as either disapproval at her hogging the menu, or maybe as a sign that Linda's thoughts have wandered back into the past again. So Harriet now leans forward, the heroine in the opera, her lines memorised, ready to mouth whatever words of sympathy she imagines Linda is shortly going to need. Linda has had her tragedy. Harriet has become good at tragedy and, rather posthumously, a professional mourner. Though without an audience. The first time Harriet tried out her act Linda told her to save her lamentations. Harriet, being the great collector of postcards, ornaments, recipes and quaint emotions that she is, was disappointed she couldn't steal a bit of Linda's sadness for her collection. However, Harriet's imagination and sense of drama being as well developed as they are, she could convince herself that Kenzo's death had a relevance to herself too. She needed the emotional reactions to the death because there's not much use in the study of Buddhism if it cannot be tested by death. Harriet had to suffer. She had to enter the temple of the spirit acquiescent, eyes lowered, the sadness of the world on her shoulders. The suffering made her look at things differently for a while, made her attractively subdued, people thought: She'd been 'a great comfort' to Kenzo's mother.

So now Harriet inclines her head towards Linda, ready to embrace her pain.

'Where will we have dinner tonight?' Linda asks on looking up from the menu.

'Oh. How about that sukiyaki restaurant. You know, the one we went to before.' Harriet has perked up, death and pain already bobbing far behind in her wake.

'Mmmm. That'd be an idea. The others won't mind I suppose.'

'No – Speaking of food, let me see the menu again.' Harriet scans the menu and at length announces she'll have a glacé-cherry tart. She sighs, leaning back in her seat. The waiter comes over reluctantly. Harriet's voice goes up three notes into her politest Japanese to order. Then giving the waiter her sweetest smile she points at some drops of water on the table to be wiped up. That done, she props her face in her hands and looks wistfully at the distant Mt Fuji. The mountain has become darker. Its red shoulder seems to tremble under the light of the sun.

Linda looks away at the mountain too, and feels bleak. What is it? This time of day she has never liked – a greyness, neither day nor night. Letting her eyes rest upon the near absolute and undisturbed mountain, Linda sinks back into the depression which began at

Kenzo's death. Her depression drifts around his death like the dull swaying of stirred sand around the place where a shark has devoured something.

She looks back at Harriet. She still believes enough in Harriet's lurid reality to imagine Harriet can somehow help her out of her blurred sadness. She wants to talk to Harriet, ask her how you can come to accept the loss of a friend.

'I hope they'll give us the second egg free,' Harriet says, rereading the menu, referring to the sukiyaki restaurant they'll be going to later.

Harriet usually needs a second egg for dipping her morsels into but grumbles at having to pay for it, which you sometimes have to, sometimes not. At the moment there's nothing on her mind except that second egg and she'd like nothing better than to occupy Linda's imagination with it too.

'They probably will, if it's the same restaurant we're both thinking of,' Linda says wearily. She could almost give up, with that egg blocking the entrance to Harriet's store of potentially sensible advice. Linda is well aware that if she could be melodramatic enough about Kenzo she could interest Harriet. Or weak enough – for Harriet loves human frailty. Harriet is so conscious of her deficiencies in certain emotions and has such a guilty jealousy of the people who do have the desired emotions, she can often be successfully approached through the object of her jealous curiosity – overt passion. But Linda wonders if it's really worth it – to be emotional, just for the sake of a bit of advice . . . it isn't.

That decided, Linda looks back at Harriet almost cheerfully, and is quite prepared to talk about second eggs or whatever to Harriet's heart's content. The waiter brings their tea and cakes. Harriet cuts her glacé-cherry tart in two with the side of her fork and tries to get a half of the cake in all at once. A large glistening crumb is stuck to the corner of her mouth. A scream is imminent? No. Harriet just gurgles as her long powerful tongue fetches back in the crumb, and then with her mouth happily full, she remarks, 'Can you imagine if we had an earthquake now? Up here – the elevators stopping and everything.'

'No, I can't,' Linda laughs, 'you'd have to scream for help. And you know the boy who cried wolf once too often.'

Harriet laughs too. 'But it should be alright up here though. These new buildings are supposed to be earthquake-resistant.'

'What about the fire?'

'I don't think we'll have to worry much about that because at the time we probably won't be in this nice safe building. You think. Divide up the twenty-four hours of the day. Okay, it's supposed to be eight hours each for sleeping, working and the rest. Think of where you are in the one place for the longest time. In bed, right? So the chances are we'd be home in bed if an earthquake hit.'

'So to be on the safe side we'd better bring our sleeping bags up here!'

Harriet grunts a laugh and looks out of the window.

Toying with her cake on its plate, Linda wonders to herself what made her so suddenly get cheerful then. She feels almost guilty. There's not much she can find to be cheerful about lately. Everything went wrong after Kenzo's death. First she had bronchitis for a month; then she went back to Sydney to try and have a holiday only to discover her father's small business had just gone bankrupt, and that all hands were needed on deck; then when she came back to Tokyo to recover from that 'holiday' she fell ill again. Still weak, she then had to work hard teaching to make up for the money she'd lost since September.

It doesn't take much remembering for the events after Kenzo's death to unreel themselves again: the stories in the newspapers, the interview with the police, the impossibility of answering Kenzo's parents' confused questions, Tatsuo's attitude about his near-drowning. Her never-ending feeling of guilty helpless inadequacy that she couldn't have been any true friend to Kenzo if she couldn't have made him feel he could open himself up to her more than he did, that she couldn't have in some way prevented his murdering and his death. But why did he do it? Why? She wants to know again. All her attempts at answers have been vague borrowings from Harriet's file of theories, one of which (out of some psychology magazine and backed up with Harriet's story about Kenzo's distant relative who had run amok and killed himself) is that Kenzo went berserk probably from some far-back hereditary imbalance of genes and brain chemicals which finally found its exacerbation and crises in the person of Kenzo. About his drowning, Harriet's idea has been that it was not the rescue-attempt mishap the inquest decided it was, but some Japanese culture atonement-suicide for having taken a life. (In other words she thought he would have killed himself that day anyway). Linda doubted the suicide idea, as she still does now, but doesn't approve of why she doubts it. She has thought again of her meditation-vision of Kenzo's death, and asks herself yet again – How could I have rung him up to say, 'Kenzo, there's some kind of "angel" trapped inside you. It hid in you to elude a demon. It's going to have to make you die to get out'? He wouldn't have believed it. And nor does she. She doesn't believe she has any psychic powers, (Zen training anyway discouraging any tendencies to the 'supernatural' or 'psychic'). She feels guiltily foolish for having had such a ridiculous vision, yet cannot help but feel just as guilty for having ignored any kind of warning-premonition. So she now does what she's been doing since September – puts the vision out of her mind (once and for all again), but without quite entirely ridding herself of the barely conscious feeling that angels, no matter how deniable, do not retreat easily once they get a foot in the door.

Tatsuo and Ricky came into Shinjuku station by the green Yamanote line. Ricky hung onto his hand-grip swaying in the clicking plastic row above the row of seated delicately grim-faced passengers. Each face was sealed into itself. Tatsuo's face, being a train-travelling Japanese face now, was also blanked-over.

The cold self-possession of the passengers was broken when the train stopped at the platform. The people rioted calmly out of the doors, the women lethal with brooch points and wedding rings. Taller than their mothers, the meat and milk-fed, bespectacled gangling children bowled past the little old ladies on the platform. Station attendants with ropes and loudspeakers corralled the mob towards the stairs and it was channelled away like flood water. Ricky and Tatsuo stumbled and bobbed somewhere in the middle of the throng, Tatsuo pushing and elbowing his way free as unflinchingly as he was punched and elbowed, it all being part of the everyday Tokyo station ritual.

They emerged into a Belshazzar's feast hall of tiered escalators and mosaiced pillars cathedralling upwards to department stores and further rail terminals thundering and echoing in the heavens of the station building. Underground shopping malls and subways vibrated beneath their footsteps over the tile floor encrusted with the black chewing gum spots which were being laboriously scraped off by uniformed crones on their hands and knees. Above the roar of the crowd were three different musak systems, store music and | 71 greetings. And even higher than they echoed the announcement, 'If anyone has found a pink plastic umbrella would he kindly bring it to the Lost Property Office as soon as possible.'

Cosmetic-masked android elevator-girls enticed shoppers into their elevators, balleted and bowed with flourishes of their white-gloved hands and then charmed the doors shut with wand-like index fingers. The elevators went up, lighter than air.

Tatsuo and Ricky moved through the technicolour air-conditioned mini-city which is Shinjuku station. Walking out of the last futuristic movie-set interior they entered a vast car and pedestrian tunnel which takes one on the last oxygen-less stages of the Odyssey towards the Sumitomo building. Receding towards the small square of light at the other end were hundreds of heads, countless heads in the great steady migration which had begun in shop A and which would end in coffee shop B.

When Tatsuo and Ricky emerged at the other end, to their dilated pupils the Sumitomo building with its sister skyscrapers seemed to crash down through the brilliant blue sky like the spokes of a war-path sun. Tatsuo and Ricky inched across the white mica plaza so wide it seemed the shadow of a cloud directly overhead could be drawn upon it. People, a few minutes before having hastened with such impudent speed through the station building, now appeared to creep with pilgrim steps across the plaza towards the doric-white skyscrapers aiming their vanishing points at the sky. Gravity dropped shadowless and heavy here. The sun multiplied in the solar disc plaza.

After an eternity of walking Tatsuo and Ricky finally reached the revolving glass doors of the Sumitomo building. Linda and Harriet were encapsulated within some restaurant slotted in near the top of that sky building. The blue sky shivered and whirled in huge rectangles through the revolving glass doors. Then, there, set in a tri-angular prism in the lobby floor of the hollow triangular building, the blue sky was again set flinging against itself throughout the diamond prism.

People, as people are apt to do with something they want to destroy but know they cannot, stepped with childlike curiosity on to the glass prism in the floor as if it could be disturbed like a pool of water. But the multiple skies and eternities of plate-glass galleries in the fly's-eye prism did not move. The people were more amazed by that simple fact than what they thought they would be. Their various investments and small change had helped build the building that contains the sky-containing prism but they could not move it. They did indeed wonder at what could move it.

Ricky and Tatsuo walked toward the elevators and stood beneath the blunt indicator-arrows alternating yellow and white. Those elevators were unattended silences which moved devoutly towards the sky as if bearing sacrifice and tribute. The extended vastness of the lobby's painting and tapestry-hung walls became two lines finally becoming one as the elevator doors closed.

'Harriet,' Linda says, 'when are the others supposed to be coming?'

'They should be here now actually.' Harriet consults her watch, staring at it as if hoping it might suggest things to talk about. Linda has gone quiet a lot this afternoon, she considers. What a bore. It's about time she should have come out of all these delayed reactions. Trust the others to be late. 'Those cream fingers look good. I'm having one. Are you?'

'No, I'll just have another cup of coffee before the others arrive.'

Harriet calls over the waiter and then dismisses him with their new order. Harriet wonders if it would be a good moment now to tell Linda that this week she won a new research grant for her Buddhist studies. She toys with the idea, carefully gauging the every moment on Linda's face, which is now staring out of the window again. Yes? No? (The little girl squatted in the corner of the garden, scratching her bottom and watching the squirmings of the little lizard which she'd nailed to a tree trunk.)

'Linda,' she begins, 'did I tell you that . . ?' Linda looks away from the window. The sun has nearly set behind Mt Fuji. The colors are rapidly fading from the sky. 'What?'

Harriet changes her mind: it's not the right time to tell her. 'Did you know that the Bunraku puppet group is coming up from Osaka next month?'

'I didn't know that,' Linda says, hardly listening.

'They are. It says here.' Harriet resumes reading her copy of *The Japan Times*.

Linda looks back out of the window. She tries to take up her line of thought again. Beneath the window the buildings are fairly clear but the farther out your eyes go – to the mountains, the details blur into one grey purple mass. The eddies, in time and space, fade out at the foothills of the mountains. To Linda, her misery one moment seems like the towering wall of a house up close, then the next, it is a wall out there, tiny, blurred in with the countless other walls, disappearing. And she becomes aware at last that if her vantage point were higher in the blue sky, the city that contains the wall of her misery would blur as a dot into the planet, and the more distantly she might retreat into the darkening sky the more of a vanishing atom would become whatever ultimately contained her divisible misery, just as her very vantage point itself would become nothing.

She strains her eyes to see better. Out there the sun has picked out a window and has made it flash gold in the deepening dusk. Without the sun it would never have been seen. It was rescued from the ever-widening obscurity by a freak sunbeam. It is like the better Kenzo. The window. Flashing for a moment. Linda saw it. Something bright. But why is it Kenzo? she wonders. She looks around at Harriet . . .

Harriet shrieks. Tatsuo and Ricky are walking across the restaurant. 'We're here. HERE!' Harriet yells, flapping her hands in the air. Ricky and Tatsuo come over smiling. Harriet suddenly turns to Linda and says quickly, 'Remind me to tell you later about the grant I got this week.'

A few hours later the four are sitting in one of Shinjuku's rococo-style coffee shops, in an underground shopping arcade on the other side of Shinjuku station.

Tatsuo leans back in his Louis XVI chair and looks up at the swirling Fragonard ceiling arching over the chandeliered salon. 'Hollywood rococo. It's all so fake it's almost real rococo anyway.' He lets issue an amiable yawn at the ceiling painting where a young lady on a swing is poised midair with a pink slipper poised on her toe. 'This is what I love about Tokyo. I brought you all here to see what real kitsch is.'

Linda gives the vase holding a carnation a scratch to see if the silver is paint. The carnation is genuine. Every table has one in a vase.

She looks about the room. Above, the stateliness of the chandeliers is being undercut by the activity of the waiters below, flying up and down the marble staircase like TV monkeys in deadly earnest mischief. In the middle of the room is a plaster Venus de

Milo holding herself a little forward over an arrangement of palms. Her features are lost in the heavy powdering of unshadowed whiteness. Young girls in stiff bright kimono are bobbing past the Venus de Milo. The girls' hairdos are polished up into little buns, their feather boas a white static electricity. They are doing a lot of stiff bright talking, pink nails brought to the lips to subdue giggling. Tatsuo and Linda are watching them in the gilt wall mirrors. Across the mirror now wriggle two hussy-types, heavily made up, in suits slit up the backs to reveal black-stockinged legs. Their faces have a hostile sensitivity, as if they are actually aware it is impossible that they could ever look that slatternly. Tatsuo makes some noisome remark about them to Linda, who promptly chokes on her coffee. Harriet obligingly thumps her on the back. Harriet hasn't seen Tatsuo for a long time, and is rather dubious about his humour. Tatsuo now speaks into the carnation as if it were bugged. Over the music system now trumpets Handel, replacing Bach. The ubiquitous Big-Sister voice on the PA hasn't yet located the owner of that pink plastic umbrella. And almost in time with the trumpet refrain the kimonoed girls toss their boas over the back of their brocaded chairs.

Tatsuo looks as if he is just about to make some comment about them. 'No . . .' Linda warns. 'Come on – Let's have a toast – It's your last night in Tokyo remember.' Tatsuo will be leaving tomorrow for California to study computer technology on a one-year scholarship.

They all pick up their glasses and toast Tatsuo.

Putting her glass down Harriet says, 'You seem to have quite an urge to get out of Tokyo,' but only implying to herself that she's jealous of his getting a grant too.

Tatsuo glares at her, looking up from his glass.

'It was so good of you, Tatsuo, to let me have your apartment,' Ricky suddenly says. 'Yes, truly.'

Tatsuo looks into his smoothly ethereal face, 'Don't mention it.'

Tatsuo had asked Linda if she knew anyone who wanted an apartment for just a year; so Linda asked Harriet, and Harriet produced one of her diaphanous carrot-juice Zen friends, Ricky, who would make the apartment 'a meditation centre of peace and sanctity'. 'It's good that you live so near Harriet, Tatsuo,' Ricky says, 'Harriet and I'll be able to coordinate very nicely . . .'

Linda puts her glass down and sits back, bored by Ricky. He's as milky-sweet about Zen as Harriet is black coffee. Both weary her intensely. All this Buddhism business. She glances at Tatsuo hoping he'll say something refreshingly cynical.

But he is silent, just listening to Ricky and Harriet talking.

Suddenly he pushes his hand through his short hair, and exclaims to Linda about the dryness of the heated air in here. 'Glad I went jogging today.'

'You're not going to get me into that again,' Linda says, seeing his smile.

'I wasn't hinting,' he laughs, holding a folded serviette against his nose.

'You've taken the last one now,' Linda scolds.

Harriet's voice is getting louder. She's making a point to the nodding Ricky which seems to require a tapping of the table edge as if it were the space bar of a typewriter.

Exchanging glances with Linda, Tatsuo mumbles something about 'Margaret Thatcher', and starts talking in an undertone about jogging and kneecaps.

'Oil of Aluminium fixes that!' Ricky says. Or Linda thinks she heard – 'Oil of Aluminium?' – Linda turns to Ricky incredulously. Ricky explains patiently: no, it's not aluminium. He brings his hands together in the air and appears to be squeezing an orange within. (He learnt how to explain things without the use of 'words' at the Zen centre.) But the mime finally has to resort to speech when he has to explain how hot the mustard-pack thing should be when you wind it around your 'abused knee'.

Linda's ears are going in two directions at once. 'My dear Harriet,' Tatsuo suddenly says, cutting Harriet short, 'the Kenzo I knew before I went away and the Kenzo who did whatever he did that night were two different people as far as I'm concerned. And that's all there is to it.' His smile is fixed, white.

'That's interesting . . .' Harriet says, her head on one side with affronted curiosity.

Chiming in with the best of Buddhist intentions Ricky asks her a question about who'll be at the midnight meditation tonight. Harriet thinks a moment, and counts off on her index finger. Tatsuo relaxes a little in his chair. And nonchalantly lights a cigarette. Linda looks at him. God, what did Harriet ask him? He's been avoiding saying anything at all about Kenzo. Since September he's been pointedly cold and off-hand about everything to do with Kenzo. She remembers the first time in September when she wanted to want to talk about it all calmly – Tatsuo abruptly stopped her, muttered something about 'histrionics', and changed the subject. He seems to have become two different people too, the one connected to Kenzo to now be regarded as non-existent. Linda often isn't sure which Tatsuo it is she is friends with. She often feels she doesn't know him at all: there is no feeling – for instance she could look at his arm, and, disturbingly for her, because of his coldness, have no feeling that Kenzo's hand had ever rested there. She doesn't like this at all. Tatsuo's providing her with only his friendship, with no inclusion of Kenzo, is not her idea of continuity.

Every now and then she glances over at his silence, his real or fabricated cheeky inviolability, and feels sad and distant from him. And meanwhile, Ricky's kindly efforts to keep Harriet's curiosity amused elsewhere are becoming more and more of a depressing effort and something which must be rescued.

Linda starts to rummage about in her bag to find small change to pay for her share of the bill. Looking around, Harriet says, 'Yes what time is it? We've got to be there by 11.45.'

'Five to eleven,' Linda says.

'Good,' Harriet picks up her glass again. 'One more toast for Tatsuo.'

Linda darts her a look to see if she's teasing, then quickly picks up her own glass to follow suit when she sees Harriet is actually trying to be nice.

Also to show goodwill, Tatsuo picks up his glass and toasts himself with a little joke at his own expense. They all laugh . . . A slight earth-tremor can be felt going through the building. The wine in the glasses quivers but the movement soon passes. 'There's your earthquake Harriet,' Linda laughs. Harriet laughs too – 'Come on let's get going . . .'

Linda continues to feel better walking with the other three to Shinjuku station. With Harriet and Ricky happily engaged in prattling away about if you should charge a small admission fee into a meditation centre, Linda says shyly to Tatsuo, 'I'll miss you.' 'I'll miss you too,' he says, giving her an obtuse smile. The long scarf around his neck makes his finely-chinned head seem set. Linda thinks to herself – Whenever it is you'll come back, I want to hear you talk. They then fall into conversation about Continental Airlines, by which Tatsuo'll be going to the States. Linda asks him if it is a direct flight.

While they talk she suddenly thinks to herself – I'm sick of myself. All this dreariness and gloom I've been in. What's happened to my sense of adventure? I'm going away too. Somewhere. Anywhere . . .

Chris and Nicky and the others are going to Chiba in two weeks time. I could meet up with them at the end of some trip by myself – North, Central Japan. I've never been there before. Tomorrow's December. I could go before the winter term at school starts . . . She feels even better, and wants to tell Tatsuo her idea. Then no, she decides, I'll go away quietly.

In Shinjuku station Ricky and Harriet stand on one platform (they're off for a midnight Zen sitting in Meguro-ku) and Tatsuo and Linda stand on the opposite platform.

Harriet's train comes in first. She leads the way onto the crowded carriage and on the seat buttocks free enough room for herself and Ricky. Comfortably seated now she twists her head around to wave goodbye to Linda. She squints hard through her short-sightedness and thinks – Is he putting his arm around her? – No – He just raised his arm up behind her to straighten his coat collar.

Linda's standing staring fixedly at the platform. Gloomy girl these days, Harriet thinks. As the train jerks out of the station Harriet hears an inexplicable tee-hee inside her head and the need to say something nasty to Ricky about Linda's forgetting to wave decreases.

Three days later, from Nagano city, Linda climbed back into the mountains by a local train then by a bus to the shoulders of the mountains. Sitting cooped up with the other people in the stuffy, over-heated carriage, Linda was keen to get as far away from people as possible, as high into the mountains as possible. She was dearly hoping it would be snowing at the top of the mountains. Had been raining in Nagano city. Rain heavier now mistier foothills thrusting up beneath the twisting and turning train. Soft umber. Soft beige. Sienna. Reddish-orange furred hills sweeping up breaking in jagged peaks swirling train the hem of a gown around them. Bearding out from bare peaks rainy mist rows and rows of fir trees stacked along the mountain sides distant carpet pile fir trees oblong patches dull beige underfelt shorn showing. Dizzied the train skirting around up around then straight through tunnel after tunnel climbing a long dark tower staircase windows let in here and there seeing sudden chasms scraps of snow –

Reaching a highland plateau the train levelled off shot through rainy dismalness to the town where Linda changed to a bus. Never ceasing the bus climbing around up through higher tumble-down villages and rice fields slipped plates arranged like rice fields.

Heavier rain diagonal wind.

Nearly giving up hope for snow just then finally horizontal rain now striated by snow pellets winding down the snow winding down around the bus a great streaking spiral ecstasy. Grinding on snow chains higher and higher the bus the last of the farmhouses blurred down away from view in the smaller, drier, determined snow flakes.

Determined. Linda's leg with impatience twitched when the person next to her started conversation talking asking pre-recorded questions supposedly friendly When did you come to Japan Why did you come? Distracting. The sight of the falling snow view cut a stranger unfair talking to you in the middle of a movie. Coming to the good part the stranger had found out all he wanted to know. The bus changing to another bus. The snow no longer falling out of the sky but up sideways everywhere in the middle of the obliterating everything Linda and her new friend no longer a nasty stranger sunk across to a new bus Heaven car for ascending up into the snow storm ascending up a winding farther mountain valley by valley decreasing upwards.

No limit. No mountain top. Goodbye to her friend Linda jumped off into through the grey ploughing to where her lodge was a vague roof line the only railing in the storming grey exquisitely alone Linda a few minutes never farther from herself alone exquisitely.

Effusive welcoming warm and intimate lodge-keeper at the swirling door Linda's heart sank. Human cheer. She'd come to stay at an aunt's it seemed. It was thrust upon her. Cheerily being led to her warm and aunty room Linda's heart sank deeper from being friendly and acknowledging the other guests' smiles. Linda annoyed at being annoyed with being friendly. A pleasant young lady after all, the lodge-keeper thought.

No sooner tossing her things into her aunty attic room than Linda was in her boots again escaping stamping up the icy screaming cloud road. Grumping at the road Linda impulsively lurching off the unseen side lurching thigh-deep in unexpected snow. A feat of stupidity. Floundering under the breaking snow wave she got back on a rock of ice and sat and stumped and emptied her boots of snow. One or two passing car faces delighted at the Linda spectacle. Ears and nose frozen Linda went back to her aunt's chastened and peaceful and tired.

At dinner she found herself wedged in between two married couples who had been seated there 'to look after her' she suspected. With her elbows locked in at her sides, in the vice of the married couples, Linda tried to get through dinner saying as little as possible. However, the young couples were not at all put off by Linda's taciturnity. Linda could have kicked herself for having forgotten that the best way to shut people up is not by being silent. Silent people attract questions. Linda then tried to quiet the couples by asking them the kind of personal question they were asking her. It worked. Silence reigned, but rigidly. But then, almost sighing aloud, Linda felt guilty for her cheeky manner and, remembering that as a foreigner she was a source of obligatory entertainment, decided to properly amuse everyone by saying the usual banalities for instance she could eat raw fish even though in Australia they

didn't.

The Linda Linda valued most got into the back seat and closed her eyes and the clown Linda took over the wheel. It was the only recourse for privacy. After dinner dominoes and video games were brought out at which Linda won through sheer spite.

Against what she thought was her will Linda thawed out and became sociable to the point she almost wasn't looking forward to going up to her room by herself at bedtime. But in her heart she felt her whole purpose in coming up here had been defeated – that was, to get away from people and slough off her gloom and think things out by herself; the goal had in fact been achieved in the prior contemplation of it; coming all the way up here was a mere signature on the document which simply proved to herself that she could carry out the acts she had promised to herself she would.

. . The next morning, waking early and restless after a hot stuffy night in the floor-heated room, Linda impatiently pushed open her ice-stuck window for some air. In that first draught of plunging air freezing into her lungs the landscape she had wanted for years to see – Below a snow garden every iced twig frozen into place. Nothing loose. Riveted for eternity. Icicles eaves down the slope. Beyond – sharp roofs, going back into eventual invisibility the depths and depths of Japan Alps the backbone holding Japan together Linda's mind together now. Breaks in blue-grey clouds sunlight areas travelling slopes spotlighting a snow region here a stand of white fir trees there a brilliance of rocks. One zooming spotlight over Linda's lodge garden coming magnesium flashed garden the every last crystal of snow and epitome of itself a white so intense it contracted the ecstasy pupils.

The light passed over the garden fell away. Linda jerked the window shut and swore with joy.

At breakfast Linda was again wedged in between the married couples but having seen what she had seen a few minutes before she could talk to them without guilt or constraint.

After breakfast another walk. Clouds clearing. Blue. Lone spotlights coming together in prolonged scorching light. A desert road she was walking it would become so searing. Couldn't even enjoy that because of the passing skiiers' stares. She had no skis. Her beanie dirty yellow, overcoat old, shabby out of place. No fashions. What are you doing up here you foreign woman without the requisite skis? There are certain props and lines for certain situations in Japan as anywhere and you are disobeying the context.

No skis only walking nobody simply strolls around mountains enjoying them you are eating with your bare hands where are your knife and fork skis? Linda you have no excuse save your physical presence and that's the accusation. Get back. Dejected, loathing the passing human face Linda went back to the privacy of her attic window a Rapunzel without any hair to lower.

. . . Under the full sunlight noon Linda on a meandering bus sliding graciously in retreat down the mountain road between glittering forests of diamond powder whereas the day before it had struggled up. On every corner the bus's turning revealed mountains revealing and unsheathing one another. A feat. A feat of thin flat diamond bus windows refracting spinning into view whole mountains big as mountains slowing down tops. Even the sight of one snow-lined branch a blade to cut away slightly rotten human complexity fat from the bone. The bone. The more she looked the more her heart was pared down trimmed away of excess until nearly nothing left the non-existent centre of the onion. The other nothingnesses. Nearly nothing left to separate them for a moment.

Waiting for another bus change behind the dazzling formalised snow and mountain facade lay nothing. Linda suspected. Yet another vista from the inexhaustible store of vistas slight perspective changes making happen. A relative vista. All Linda had to do was close her eyes and it would disappear. But when she opened them again the landscape nearly rumbled and echoed with its inviolable sense of its own existence. Its presence, because of its presence, strived to deny Linda out of existence as much as she tried to will it away too. But a true struggle didn't develop. She walked a little way and then looked with uncertainty back over her shoulder to see if the fabulous panorama had encroached an inch. She turned around completely and confronted it. It was still as far away from her as her shadow. An appetite for extremes satisfied profoundly with the renewed urgent whiteness and every intact screwed-in detail. A fluorescent-white marking underlining everything, underlining the fact that the landscape signified itself and nothing else, after all.

But after all the snow dunes could have been sand dunes too. Sydney childhood wind-streaked sand dunes. Both shaped by wind. It didn't matter. A reverie of reminiscence about childhood passions oceans. A love of surf and snow. Pure states monochrome absolutes to be aspired to. Human obscurity all the more obscure for the contrast. This snow landscape decisive, it couldn't have been whiter save in madness Linda craved its evaluating absoluteness its impossible extremeness by which she could've been realised if she'd stayed still long enough.

But another view another feeling. The elusive sense of easily forgotten yet perpetual freedom – that quick blink and shift of focus reminded the landscape again of its always imminent beauty of self-abandoned yet utterly self-contained grandeur. How Linda always wanted to be. It couldn't be all just rock ice and sky. There had to be a god or a Buddha behind it. The vista asked for God for Linda to have an uncomplicated awareness of it that there had to be a God in it as natural as the vista itself pantheistically. Was there God there? He said yes she thought with self-dialogue unnecessary burden a little too much justification so God decreased and it became more like ice rock and sky.

The landscape didn't change, but. Gradually counter-balancing creeping suspicions of her inspired thoughts just then were pseudo-mystical self leg-pullings sentiments as meringue as snow once the melting sun had risen high enough in the sky. After all beneath snow is soil. It all washes away bit by insidious bit, it all passes away nothing fixed Linda noble passions lives thoughts passing away the rock below the soil bit by bit replaced passing rather sanely disgusted and sobered Linda got on the bus. And the grumpy dozing driver woke up.

Out of the going-down bus windows dazzling trees and fields which were dazzling trees and field could be seen. As the bus descended the mountain reunited itself valley by valley with the other mountains which in turn came down to larger and larger villages holes began fraying in the lower snow until again the brown earth became a space greater than the snow it was engulfing and Linda's consciousness was a cut-out card mountain the pinnacle of which was being swept out of and under her view by other mountains higher than the ones behind it the farther down she descended in the heavenless car to scraped brown valleys where it would be and was already becoming a bitter vanity to maintain any image of the illusory freedom ecstasy and grandeur the illusory snow had created in a carefully chosen moment of malicious inspiration.

One freezing night in Aomori city, Linda, in her oppressively clean and comfortable hotel room, got fed up with herself and put on a coat and went to a disco. She danced with energy. Conscious of her foreign attractiveness, she knew it was going to be only a matter of minutes before someone homed in on her. As she danced she vowed again to herself that she was going to fuck someone that night. In that very singular sense of purpose she at least felt free.

When she realised she was being danced into a corner by a beaming and moustached young man she let herself be pressed into that corner and as the man's tongue went into her mouth she thrust her hips at his hips and worked her still dancing legs through the man's legs.

Within ten minutes they were both in the tub of his hotel-room's bathroom. Linda happening quickly. Unvirginly. Glider skimming over terrains of action she had previously trudged through she led the way pushing the cheery talkative man back through the paint-peeling doorway down on the bed knotting herself over him fixing him with vice-legs riding the man she could have crushed him the rearing horse she had become. In the few seconds before the man realised who was on top and before his penis started to go soft at that thought Linda jerked him off and thumped an orgasm into herself. She fell off his soft body victorious but then had to figure out how to make him feel as if he were still a man. The dark room concealed her disdain as she looked down at the man's hairless thighs, his bent dribbling penis, and his little pudding balls. With aloof sympathy she contrived to let herself lie back how a woman is expected to and let her breasts spread out like those in all those comic-book pictures of Western women the man's head was probably stuffed with. She tilted up her thighs and began the tide-going-out motions which draw the man out of himself towards the woman. She made not a sound but he gasped and cried out as if he had an audience and shot himself into her again where she wanted him to get lost and never find his way back to himself again.

When he finally slopped out of her Linda felt deeply bored but satisfied for she had achieved an inch of what she had set out to achieve. Now all she had to do was tolerantly put up with his talk and compliments about how attractive she was. She could make him do or say anything. He got her cigarettes, made her coffee and made her feel perfectly unlike the swamp she'd long felt like. She announced it was time to go to sleep. He obeyed.

Glad of her retrieved privacy she lay facing the wall thinking of how unattractive the man's body was but nevertheless feeling rather grateful for his easy shallowness. Now she wanted to leave him and this hotel but knew it would require less exhaustive explanation and lies to just lie there beside him until the morning would release her.

Since their room's window faced right onto another building the room was still dark at ten o'clock in the morning. Linda was gladly surprised when she looked at her watch and saw it wasn't early after all. Without feeling guilty she could now leave. As she tried to struggle out of the heavy quilts the man woke regrettably refreshed and tried to knead Linda's body into a fuckable shape again. She wearily let him have his fun. He fluttered her around the thin edge of another orgasm but his awkward lack of continuity made her feel itchy and ticklish. She gave herself the choice of slapping his face or brushing her hair. She chose the latter after a moment of tantalising indecision. As she sat brushing out her matted hair she looked down at the man's mouth affixed between her legs. His body hung out of her like some laughable appendage. And she actually did laugh, softly. He looked up at her and smiled back, thinking how lovable she was.

When they walked outside into the icy street Linda could have gulped down the huge, fresh, cold blue sky. She felt she could have galloped like a horse away from that stuffy little room. Had never loved the clarity of the sky as much as she did on coming out of that hotel.

After a pointless cup of coffee together Linda said goodbye to the man and threw away his name-card. Walking back towards her own hotel she realised she had rather liked the man after all and felt thoroughly pleased with herself for having victoried over and vindicated something in herself that previous night. But, the farther down the street she walked the more uncertain she became of having vindicated anything, and the more the thing was supposedly vindicated the more it seemed to refract again in the crystal eyes of the people she was passing.

For he hadn't been Kenzo, had he?

And Linda arrived in the near apex north Sapporo in Hokkaido on December nine. December ten the Kitsune Shrine's purification rite after a bus train ride into the early afternoon zero snow covering the | 85 whole landscape even the waiting in the main street of the village rugged up to their ears Linda too her iced skull. Her finger joints aching in the two pairs of gloves in her overcoat pockets. Dancing from foot to foot. Everyone smilingly indifferent to the foreigner's presence. Glad she hadn't brought her camera. Moodily regretting it all freezing in this street with its Coca-Cola and comic-book vending machines.

Something finally made the crowd move to proceed down the street Linda stiffly too, and the police and the fire departments too. To with Linda try to catch a glimpse of the white-robed rite participants ahead of the Shinto priests ahead of the crowd made its way with a certain ascertained measured dignity through the bright red Shinto Torii arch taking the eye down to a second arch closer to the water's edge Linda unobtrusively trying to catch a glimpse.

Linda was always trying to catch a glimpse. Now right behind the stiff wing-sleeved priests and their charges the white-clad young men who had been for the previous week in the temple practising the austerities Linda wanted to do but didn't but at least she had good examples in front of her now.

Actually one of the youths looked a bit like Kenzo Linda proved imagined dismissed to herself distressed at the thought of it. But that youth wasn't looking at her but at the small images of the Gods of Rice, Mountains, Shrines and Good Luck they were carrying. White everywhere the colour of purity. Hair coverings, snow, robes, folded papers between the teeth to prevent earthly breath from defiling sacred images in once again white, white and white again.

Then, how it is in Japan, after nothing seeming to have happened for a long time everything took place at once with a swift frenzy of poised containment. The white robes' belts flew away the priests stepped forth to slip off white robes from the youths revealing naked except for tight loin-clothed skins revealing goose bumps. Linda got goose bumps too. Her eyes widened at the sudden lightning of lithe brown tenseness striking down the beach the starkness the whiteness and the snow. And the water's edge holy being waded into thigh-deep by fervour, concentration, and furrowed brows Linda shivered she was seeing what she wanted to see burying her gloved hands deeper her heart bursting it didn't matter if he looked like Kenzo the youths with a shock and movement lowered carefully the images of the gods into the sea the Winter sea. It was shocking and moving. The images of the gods being apparently purified verified justified realised placated dipped in the salt of the sea the indisputability. Linda simplicity. The black volcanic sand showing through the snow being treaded back up by no visible religious ecstasy but only by relief and resolve. And pain.

It was only just beginning in Linda's tightening brows. The crowd parted with awe and the youths passed through dripping. They were followed to the shrine where they cracked the ice on the stone basin of holy water and dashed water over their heads. Over the end of the ritual Linda didn't see that part of it for she had straggled as a willing sacrificial lamb gazing at the disappearing mark on the water the youths had made. And then she was religious and thirsty and wanted to drink the seawater but there was not a drop to drink of course. It was all irreconcilable. There was stoicism and astringent aesthetic ethic to be had but it would not lend Linda any part of it it was closed away in the book of the sea the waves shutting again folding away what they had done to the images of God the Salt, a grain of salt about herself her inadequacies was all that was given to Linda after all as she was led away.

Chilled exhausted orphaned unknown she docilely sat on the bus back to Sapporo.

In her hotel room, the next morning, in the sun coming through the large windows, Linda was loosening the soil around the room's pot plant with a hotel kitchen fork. It was peaceful and relaxing. Gently digging, she envied the soil its pot, the definite containing shape of the pot. Soil was gathered for the purpose of allowing a plant to grow. A fine purpose. The pot had a rim. If soil went outside the rim it would be considered spilt, and would be either swept away or sprinkled back into the pot, unlike Linda if she were to go outside her rim, the human rim not being a definite pot rim.

Warmed by the sunlight, and slowly washing the simple abiding sensuality of the earth out of the fork's prongs under the bathroom tap, she thought how an enjoyment of the physical is the best preserver of sanity. She thought of her most rested moments in the past – the deep ease of Sydney beaches, the clouds drifting across the surf . . . Moving relaxed around her room, tidying here and there, almost getting too relaxed, she felt her peacefulness becoming depression again. So she thought to go outside before she'd start becoming a swamp again.

She went out.

Going down the street, her refreshed strides lengthened in the crisp air. A few people staring at the spectacle of a foreign woman out by herself walking but Linda in Japan long enough to be oblivious appreciating only the cold cirrus-scratched sky and the wedges of snow in the leaves of the bushes by the way walking along. In two months time the wedges of snow would all be put together as giant clowns and castles for the February snow festival. Pity it wasn't now.

After ten minutes or so a group of fifteen- or sixteen-year-old high school boys rollicking over some object of fun at which Linda's eyes in anticipation lit up coming closer the source of the boys' merriment. She saw that the tallest and largest member of the group was with one hand pelting with snow a kitten trying to escape along the side of the masonry wall. With his other hand then swung his school bag banging the kitten up against the wall. The leader now swinging the kitten by its tail over his head sent it flying into a carton in a rubbish heap nearby. The kitten mute all the while not even a peep. Plugged thrust into a high voltage socket a pure one instinct rage Linda was in front of her thoughts before she thought about it shredding into the boys' laughs with her most abusive Japanese. Words white face bloodless shouting in the middle of the street until the newly abashed boys slunk sidled off. But she didn't stop she couldn't find the kitten Fuck what have you done with it she couldn't find it. Fury stoking fury she could have punched them taken them all on punched Buddhism in the face for just sitting there. She gave up and crashed trembling off her brain on her way to the station to buy a paper how she'd intended to but the paper was full of violence too as usual – the jews the blacks the crippled the anybody. You can't do anything about it it's the way of the world it's life That's Life and Karma they say but no it isn't no more smarmy Karma Linda coming back down the steps encountered the beginning to laugh boys again the last straw she screwed down into a frigid rage and asked them as slowly as she could if they were human. Yes they were human that was the problem the cruelty cruelty of the world a funny foreigner had tried to stamp it out. The boys had stopped only

88 | because she was a funny foreigner to stop and look at . . .

Linda stamped off and the tears stamped out of her eyes back in her room sick to the pit of her stomach. For the rest of the day all day on the bed sipping gin wanting to take a punch at someone and the kitten had disappeared and nothing could be done about it they say but she had inadvertently done something about herself. The clear line where thinking ends where action begins had been rarely glimpsed. A look through a telescope where stars are clear no rims where action begins where action must begin where things begin and begin and never stop beginning for that's where the end of back seats are tossed on the pyre to fuel the beginning.

But oh so fleetingly. Once you'd hit the next day the beginnings of anything were lost in rail and bus terminals in Hakodate, Nemuro, Otaru or anywhere. She was beginning to get lost in confusions of tickets bags and drinks in bars up through Hokkaido to Wakkanai the top of Japan where you can see the USSR across the Sea of Okhotsk. Poised up there on the geographical limit of her trip on the bleak grey cliff behind her Tokyo started to reel her back in down Japan again across the Tsugaru Straits on a stormy ferry from Hakodate Japan drinking her down like her glass of whisky she kept seeing before her eyes never-ending bottom of forgetting best intentions irresolution and despair and wondering where she'd gotten to. Dreams hallucinations dreams didn't know who she was who she'd be. Couldn't come soon enough meeting up with Chris and Nicky down in Chiba. At least she didn't have to drink by herself anymore.

Now standing on a Chiba beach they were watching their shadows movie-screened onto the surf by the headlights of their van back on the beach road. Linda had never seen such a sight before – the waves breaking under her apostle-like shadow's feet out beneath the richly starred sky. Watching that unusual effect made the group alternately silent then talkative. They watched for a long time, until they got cold.

They went back to the beach house and Chris poured drinks. Everyone began drinking steadily. The more they drank the louder the talk and laughter got. Rock music went on Reg shoved the sofa back. Wine was tipped over. Dancing. Someone berserk slid down the internal staircase bannisters while Chris pushed foam mattresses over the internal balcony rail onto the dancers below.

Chaos noise dancing bouncing dancing pulling a fishing net off the wall deliriously Linda threw it over Nicky then Reg dragged her laughing around the floor like a mop hoarse laughing her high spirits were rimless no past no future everything wonderfully spilt.

Until four-thirty in the morning the bacchanal continued until everyone fell into their beds horizontal sinking into sleep. Coming up a few hours later staggering around and still laughing and making brunch bananas and bacon and slicing bread all over the place. Eating brunch someone played back a tape of last night's furor no one else knew was going. All the roaring laughing again her mouth full of banana she was laughing again thinking you can enjoy things twice it was fascinatingly repulsive fascinating.

Brunch after brunch they pushed one another into the van to go to the Nichiren temple in the mountains in the middle of the Boso peninsula a bit of sightseeing. The speed of the van made Linda feel prematurely throttled hurtled towards some kind of climax to her trip the end of her trip. Only one last stage of her trip left now – back to Tokyo one hundred kilometres away. The last leg. Such a journey around Japan without a climax would be incomplete wouldn't it she nearly shrieked passing the vermouth flask. She looked at the way the scenery passed as if something in it might help her gag herself, all scrunched up her legs going to sleep.

The van stopped at the foot of the cliff on which a small shrine overlooked the Pacific Ocean. Glad of the chance to stretch the legs and have an icecream. They all climbed the perilous stone steps roughly to the shrine. For a joke Linda was wearing Japanese clogs – high wooden horse's hooves platforms which rocked and tripped Linda up the path to the lookout where she strode and frisked. A low wire fence separated the lookout area from the narrow strip of the cliff edge. A bit of drama for a change two of the group stepped over the fence to look at the ocean beneath. The surf the white the rocks. Alcohol on her breath Linda compelled to follow to totter about in clogs on the cliff edge she'd always dreamed of. The surf the rocks, mermaids the end. The more the others told her to come back the more she tottered lurching about laughing crying certainly she didn't want to jump but wanted to shriek her throat to ribbons God I loved you Kenzo you bastard. As a woman. As a fucking woman. Too late. Was it all ever more than that? That Buddhism infatuation. Shit.

She tottered about crying and laughing she didn't want to jump but there was that barely suppressed hope the cloth might be pulled at any moment from under her by accident. However, the anticipating of a thing automatically disqualifying its spontaneity there was nothing Linda could do but get back over the fence.

Back in the van they drove for an hour downing beer and eating peanuts nearly hitting posts until they came to Nichiren's famous temple high in the cirrus mountains. Linda had passed through moods of garrulousness and irritable silence. The others gave up.

Now wending their way through the magnificent groves and lanes of the temple there was again that sense of imminent pseudo-climax. The lack of synthesis to the trip made the trip a chamber without a key. Linda urgently chased on, up through the dignified verifications of the magnificent avenue of thousand-year-old cedar trees, hungry and crazed for a revelation she knew would never manifest.

Then. Up ahead, at the last turn of the path he was walking, Reg called out come and look at this. What? On the spur of the moment as yet unseen by Linda was around the last corner of one of the paths a newly erected concrete extravaganza Indian stupa put up by the modern Nichiren Buddhism sect.

Linda staggered forward with a beer in her fist. As sacrilegious as everything else. One of the paths through the gold sun shadowed cedars suddenly dropped, turned and widened to the corners of the eyes the flung horizon astounding encompassing with immense theatre the huge white stupa pointed at the sky beyond the sky containing the Buddha bone, the bit of ash. The blue-line frieze around the dome. One sweep of sky and sea. One sweep of mountains. The sun making it all exist, visible. Sea mountain sky sun focused by the stupa yet the stupa a giant white fondant white elephant joke of Neo-Buddhism. The elements stretched wide high and far to disown it to make it disappear. The horizon had escaped so far only a distant haze where it had been was left. The elements of the heavens set against themselves in a perfectly harmonised, parallel and plausible joke. The onion dome its quasi-infinite layers mocking the universe right down to the place in the centre where there was no bone, no ash at all. Only the spirit of the thing was left but that had gone as far as the eye could see.

Part
Three

Harriet is finishing off her dinner. She is toying with the remains of a cheese and bacon pie. In the warm evening air the brandy liqueur chocolates are going a bit soft on their plate. The butter has soaked somewhat into the last slice of rye bread which Harriet has temporarily forgotten . . .

She is enjoying dinner by herself, that's how she likes it, on this humid July night, with the French windows open. And nearby, there are so many books to be opened, records to be lifted up and put down again, and soft thin curtains to be drawn back as far as possible to let in the every breeze. A breeze on a night like this is a cool skin on the milk, ages having been taken for it to form.

Sitting on a large cushion on the floor by the low table, Harriet is turning the damply crackling pages of the newspaper before her. Long and heavy, her breasts are resting on the top fold of her stomach. She is wearing a pink pyjama top, open in the front, and jeans giving off a faint odour of sweat and Pear's baby soap. The television is on, but without the volume. Low music is coming from a small cassette-player, so low only the highest flute notes can be heard.

Looking up at the TV now and then, Harriet files ner nails and thinks about maybe phoning Linda, who hasn't phoned her for some time. Linda now works at Harriet's school, but they teach different days. The nail file is the diamond powder kind. The sharp sensation of it going across the tops of her nails is somehow a perfect accompaniment to her feeling of drowsy well-being. Harriet never uses nail polish but attends carefully to manicuring. She now applies the file to her toenails. They are so hard, however, she has to leave off reading to grip her toes one by one to file them.

Finishing off the last toe she sits, vaguely tired, frog-like, at the bottom of the room. She lets the images of the TV screen hold her eyes. The nail file slides sleepily down to the carpet. Her hand moves unconsciously to her jeans' zipper . . .

No. She stands up. Marches over to the TV and switches the

channel. She gets her bit of rye bread and takes it over to the French windows to chew while looking out into the dark garden.

The breeze is so light the camellia bush leaves seem to stir by themselves. The moon admires the leaves which glisten on the neck of the birch tree. The roses, as if holding their breath, seem to slowly exhale on the next breeze. The perfume, diluted by the air, is crisp and light in Harriet's nostrils. She breathes it down slowly . . . Standing there, comfortably slouched, she feels the faint jolt of an earth tremor pass under. A reflex part of her mind relocates to itself the cupboard where her earthquake-kit bag is kept. She nearly has a wonder about what she'd do if a strong quake were to ever hit, but she feels too listless and relaxed to think about it too hard. Anyway, the tremor has already subsided.

Large moths, laden with powder, wade through the air towards the livingroom lights. Harriet fights down a scream as a floury moth pushes past, and sneezes instead. The sound stirs the garden. A cloud covers the moon as if to protectively darken the garden's eyes. The garden sinks back into itself. Fold into fold of shadow, the cat curling further into the bush, the worms coiling deeper into the soil, it will never know what disturbed it.

Something stirs in the warmest part of her bowels. Harriet goes to the toilet. She isn't there long as she dislikes the actual defecation.

Leaning against the mantlepiece again, away from the moths coming in the door, though still able to see the garden, Harriet yawns and lazily lifts the singing trophy on the mantlepiece. It is one of her prizes from her undergraduate days. Setting it down again, closer to the vase, she thinks she really ought not to have let her singing go . . . The room seems to yawn too now. It is a good yawn, bored and satisfied. She is more physically relaxed these days, meditating every day. Though aware she is not what is called attractive, Harriet likes her body and has full ownership over it. A jealous body, hoarding whatever its senses can take in. But greed is its only fault. Harriet is not vain and has only a perfunctory use for mirrors. She can easily forget her body; she is seldom ill. Her body just follows her mind along. Her mind – it has little connection with her body. It is a thing of one immaculate essay leading into the next, one seized scholarship preparing the way for another. Her mind can never forget itself. It is as calm as a computer, distilling whole books of knowledge to decimal points, squeezing the moisture from the carbon until it is diamond-brief, unscratchably specific. All mind and body, her heart is just a tenant in her being. She spares it nothing. It has few memories. But it's there, and sometimes has its own little voice, in the quiet of the night.

The room yawns again. Harriet is bored and contented. She'll give herself an early night – the perfect touch to the rare holiday she has given herself today. She won't be bothered with tidying up. She'll just take off her jeans and lie under the sheet as she is.

So the room is passed through – the fat to congeal under the broken cheese crust in the dish, the chocolates to harden again in the cooler midnight air, the phone not to be rung after all, and finally, the ants to converge in long relentless lines upon the table in the centre of the room.

Throughout the spring and summer Linda thought she was doing just fine, not thinking or feeling too much anywhere, anytime; putting Buddhism and emotional dramas a million years ago, working, watching TV, being social, going out, but kicking the heavy-drinking habit; just getting along, doing fine, looking forward to the any and every opportunity to have fun like in the good old days.

For it is hot. It is July. Eleven lusty English teachers with nine Japanese go charging into the mountains for a day's outing. A bus rollercoasting through the hills. Hills flung along the sky. Butterflies doing cartwheels through the air. Old women looking up, bra-less under summer kimonos. Sunburnt children scuffling with the foreigners in the village shop to buy icecreams, teeth-rotting Cokes, lunches and beer.

They walk up the mountain road, straggling as rainbow-painted sheep. The sky is drenched to its belly with blueness and warmth. The mountains, a grease-paint green, arc higher and higher behind one another. They climb into the sky only to climb back down again on the other side.

Linda and Chris walk together as they are friends. Nicky has a person beside him too – a quiet boy, his new lover. Beside them all, churning, broken up white on the staircase of rocks is the river they'll be swimming in later, further upstream. Whenever they get there. For they're straggling, rambling, melting icecream down their wrists, beer cans opening exploding fountains that get Linda up the backs of her legs on purpose. She stamps with laughter in her army boots, flicks Nicky with her beach towel and gets the zinc cream on her nose messed. Chris pulls her hair out of her zinc cream for her but pinches her on the bottom with the other hand.

They reach halfway up the hill. Cool tree shades swim down and loose parasols of ferns turn past. Legs brushing. Splashed deer skin through upwards shadows. They are quiet. Nothing but rock tearing blazing silk out of the water can be heard. Someone wants to swim. But not yet. Too deep, too fast. They move upwards towards groups of picnickers. Then they get lost when half the group stops off at the toilets. Linda and Chris and an Englishman stick together, wandering up the road calling through the valley for the others. Down the road careful not to run for they are nearly drunk. The sun flits in the sky. The Englishman doles out the beer, Linda the jokes.

Found again they are escorted up and down over dangerous bridges waterfalls ravines down down to a tiny pebble beach behind the knee of the mountain on the river. The others are halfway through lunch. Linda yells curses at Nicky for not waiting for them. He yells back.

Chris has forgotten his lunch. Poor Chris, so Linda sits him down and feeds him out of her lunch box. Savoury cold meat, rice and sesame seeds and grapes as dark and fat as pearls. She is kind. Chris well knows it. They giggle and whisper as conspirators on their share of the pebbles. Chris could almost kiss her. Too late! Nicky stands up to unveil himself. Mr America rises glorious in Cardin bathing trunks. He leads the faithful to the water. They plunge in like lemmings. He remains on the pebbles. Linda hoots with laughter. The blue and chilled creatures nevertheless reach the other side to raise themselves up and jeer back. It looks like fun. Linda wriggles out of her clothes to reveal pebble-marked thighs and hard pointed tits under her bathing costume. Scoops her hair up around her head. Wades in. Leg and neck muscles stand out against the torrent. The river is falling down the mountain taking tons of gravel with it so why not Linda? They wave goodbye to her. Downstream she clambers, a drunken and sodden mermaid, onto a large rock to accept the applause coming downstream. In a quiet and deep and blue corner of water she performs dives. Wonderful straight-through dives. The audience clambers along the bank downstream bearing homage of whisky and fruit.

Holding the base camp is the Englishman conjuring tea out of a miniature stove that works on solid kerosene. Lemon slices flash through the air. Sugar twinkles in the palm as crushed stars. Chris helps him drink the tea and hears funny stories about London.

Shortly Chris joins the group lolling paganly on the rock downstream to applaud the water-ballet star Linda. Whisky and grapes are spilt on the rocks. Brown flesh arabesques with beach towel colour and they are all full and happy and exhausted.

The sun shifts. The trees lurch. A squadron of small clouds has led a massed formation over the gorge. The clouds round and thicken with thunder. Sharp rain drops pit down. A united shriek rises from the pagan rock. Linda, towel-girt, leads her tribe off the rock and across the steaming pebbles.

Bag, bottle and lemon slice crowd and fluster one by one up a step ladder to safety. An unlocked mountain cabin is found. The group pushes in, makes a new picnic on the dusty floorboards, tosses back wet hair and wraps around towels against the tempest. Food stuck with grass and sand is sorted out on the floor. The whisky and beer go around. All hell breaks loose. The Englishman has started up a game with the loser having to drink a capful of alcohol. There are more losers than winners. Linda shows all her fillings screaming with laughter a savage pounding the floorboards with her bare knuckles. Chris shies off a bit, but he is soon sucked back into the vortex of her hysteria.

The rain abating, they troop back down the dusk mountain. Linda does a flamenco in front of a truck. Whistles. In the bus shelter they hand out whisky to the old couple waiting there. Soft chocolate. Somebody, in a floppy pink hat sits in the bus driver's seat pretending to start up. The real driver nearly has to call the police to get him out. Down the mountain they go. Chris pulls Linda's breast and she bites his hand. They scuffle and laugh and Linda jumps into the aisle. Where she breathes and calms down. Then she finds herself sitting next to Nicky's boyfriend Misa.

He says to her softly, 'Kenzo told me all about you.'

And she felt it yet didn't know she felt it – The angel, invisible, moved away. Been watching all along.

Harriet is trying not to groan as she dreams. She is a small thing but big unto herself, a shocking pain pierced right through her breast. But she lives, she is determined to survive this. The bark of the tree is cool and smooth under her. She twists her body but she is nailed. How long has she been like this? Time is different, faster and longer for a creature her size. If she jerks her head around a bit she can see a distant looming and receding blur. A huge thing comes forth to press the nail in further. A great swimming watery eye with a black dilating and contracting centre set in a circle of grey-green comes closer. To do what? To see better.

Frantically jerking and squirming this way and that. Rage and pain and bewilderment and fear and the instinct to survive somehow nailed to the great tree now soaring up through the universe. Fixed forever. A little girl finger prods her. Then picks its nose as it watches.

Even the universe is powerless to stop Linda from dreaming she is a nail, the blade of a knife, the plug of a volcano, the bit of plutonium in a H-bomb. Then she is the thing nailed, the thing knifed, the thing exploded, the thing destroyed. She is America. She is Hiroshima. She is eating quail in a space ship. Eating rice in a temple. She is being born. Being dead. Dreaming a dream not her own seeing a horizon her heart knifed through. Nibbling Harriet's leg. Flashing glittering glass doors turn. Revolve and stop. For an instant the sky opens and blinks and shuts. A white bird pursued by a black bird hides inside Kenzo. The danger passed it struggles to get out. The only way out to crash the cage to the ground and fly out the broken door. It is gone. Beginning to turn again the revolving doors spin to a blur of invisibility. A car passes the room.

Counterpoint slice slop slur buzz laughing humming crying whispering muttering nothing can be heard. Can be heard. Can be seen. Nothing. She remembers nothing she wakes up she dreamed but nothing happened. She hits her pillow softly cracklingly it rustles nothing empty Pandora's box she peers over at the alarm clock. Too early to get up it hasn't rung yet but she does.

Jeans t-shirt. Open the window to let the air in. Warm damp summer air. Smoggy today. Little can be seen. Falling into the kitchen. The first woman on Mars. The first feeling as strange and cold underfoot as that.

A headache. Two aspirins. Has a shower. Can't remember what she has to do today but something important surely. Never mind.

What about breakfast.

Cold rice clotted in the bottom of the pot. Move it. Another spoon needed to get the mess off the spoon. Stuck in a bog. She is congealed in the bottom of this morning. It is hard to move. The haunted yellow chill of the open fridge. Scratching around for the butter. Picking at the white bread more preservative than flour. This is raw morning. Could fall down between the cells of the bread and hallucinate suicide at the bottom of the chasm. Oh but not this morning. It's out of the question. People have to be met, buses caught, air breathed. Must do it Must move Must eat nothing but Must keeps us going. Must is a wonder drug. Hack the butter as if it were a bit of wood. Agitate the rice grains apart with a gas flame underneath. Get coffee powder in your cuticles. Let the sugar rain on the floor for all I care.

Stop short. That's enough. Time to climb back onto the conveyor belt and move towards the Toy factory. Time to put on a face, give the day a kick in the arse to get it going, begin circling like a sheep-dog around the straggling hours and get them herded tidy into the pens of the days. The world won't stop for me as I stand here, leaning against the fridge, chewing a cud of bread and rice.

Now I remember, today's the day I'm going to meet Misa.

A hush descends. Everything suddenly seems wider and more spacious. There is room to move. I can go this way or that way. Heaven and Earth allow me. I know whom I'm meeting at precisely eleven this morning. We will have lunch and talk. He's a nice person. He's quiet and gentle. He knew Kenzo. Knew him in a way I never knew him. Therefore he is my route to Kenzo. Sitting beside Misa, if I accidentally brush his arm while passing something I'll be touching skin which has touched Kenzo's. Living skin with the shadow of dead skin still upon it. A particle of Kenzo's breath may still be in his lungs. Misa's. Misa. What are we going to say to each other? We can't of course talk directly about what we want to talk about as that would be rude and over-curious and breaking all the rules so we'll make do somehow and hedge around it. But I'm nervous of meeting you. In fact I'm a little frightened. I'm frightened of being disappointed by you or by what you'll say for after all what can you possibly tell me that I don't already know? But I hope there is something, I really do.

of Tokyo. From the windows the nape of Tokyo's dirty neck can be seen. But Misa is sitting staring at the floor. It's 1.55. Maybe he'll be a bit late for his part-time job. It's not often he's late though – a punctual person who sticks by all the rules, a simple and unornamented twenty-two year old. His guiding line in behaviour is – you don't do to others what you wouldn't like having done to yourself – a plain and effective enough bit of Confucianism for his needs, his lack of years having yet to challenge the principle.

He's an unobtrusive, quiet young man, neat and clean as a house cat. His family runs a small home-factory business which turns out such things as washers for taps and little plastic cutters for opening plastic bags which are designed to be opened anyway without the use of gadgets. He studies traditional ceramic design at a small college in Meguro-ku. He studies hard. Life is steady and regular enough for Misa.

Except perhaps for his love-life.

It is partly because he has been lately feeling rather like some tissue pulled out of a box by his boyfriend Nicky to be briefly used and then discarded that Misa's thoughts have turned to past days when he didn't feel quite so misused. Though he sees Nicky often and though Nicky lavishes him with all sorts of gifts (which are embarrassingly obtrusive things like loud cuff-links and cut-glass whisky decanters for which Misa has little use, and anyway being passed-on leftovers from Nicky's store of tributes he has received from his own older lovers), Misa can never feel completely easy with Nicky.

Thus, disenchanted with Nicky, Misa has found himself thinking more and more of Kenzo. He knows Kenzo is dead, Nicky having told him the story with relish since Nicky was one of the last people to see Kenzo and the boy Kuni alive.

Misa remembers Kenzo clearly. He would like to remember him even better. From the beginning of the trip into the mountains he knew who Linda was, but he was too shy to approach her by herself. He certainly didn't expect her to so quickly ask to see him again. He liked her though, and at lunch today he found he liked her even more. He asked her if she would teach him English (in part to help him cope with Nicky). She readily agreed. They didn't talk about Kenzo much; but he hadn't really expected to.

The train's rounding the curve into Kawasaki station. Misa looks at his watch again – No, he probably won't be late for work, fortunately.

Linda is still sitting in the restaurant. She is sitting in front of a cup of coffee, so hard and concrete, the rose design on it too vivid and red. Lunch with Misa was pleasant, and, ultimately relaxing; but the effects of last night's poor sleep are catching up with her: depressed, surrounded by a garish whirl of silver, aprons, rouged faces, potted palms and clawing voices, she feels she is still waiting for somebody or something, but what she doesn't know.

Through the autumn Misa came to Linda's apartment once a week for an English lesson, for which Linda refused payment. His company came to be enough. Quiet and modest, Misa had no sexual attraction for her, and that suited her fine. To Misa Linda became something of a confidante who counselled him on how to deal with her other friend, Nicky, and a vivifier in his otherwise sober life. For Linda Misa was an unupsetting reassurance of the more pleasant aspects of normality. He was a stability.

There was little elsewhere. She had to find out, seek, again. She started to randomly read and experiment her way through Yoga, diet, Astrology, a bit of Shinto, north-shore Sydney-style Scientology, and even Christian Fundamentalism; everything except Buddhism. She eventually rejected each one of them individually, as she had Buddhism, as any self-contained, self-complete end in itself, but accepted parts of all of them syncretically.

Then for kicks she'd light sparklers on the balcony at two in the morning, spend hours slicing cucumbers paper-thin for pickles then not do the washing-up for weeks, suddenly decide to throw a party at midnight, and go out jogging at dawn without her Alien Registration Card and be picked up by the police and have to be identified as Linda at the police-station by some hapless sleepy Chris or Misa.

One morning she'd be the essence of self-assurance – putting on lipstick, screwing on earrings, winding up her watch and stepping decisively onto the bus to go to work, then the next day she'd sleep in, a half-eaten bit of toast under her pillow and a tampon floating in the unflushed toilet, and feel that daily life was something she could never be reconciled with.

The thirtieth of December. Tatsuo is sleeping with his head on the cold inner window of the jet from San Francisco. Nobody knows he's returning. He decided that once back he'd wait for a while before contacting anyone. But he is now dreaming he is looking forward to seeing Linda again, after all this time.

She puts the phone down. Misa'll be coming over for a pre-New Year's Eve drink. Her breath is coming out white in the cold air so she turns her second heater on. That, with the stove going, should be enough, she thinks. Giving the pot on the gas ring a stir, Linda sings a few bars of some song and flicks on the air vent fan above the stove. Her eye tries to find again the place on the recipe for carrot pickles which Harriet gave her to try out.

It starts – Up through the table legs and her own legs. A chill shoots across her breast. The glass doors of the cupboards are now smacking in their runners. The salt-shaker jiggles off the shelf onto the floor. Linda stands frozen gripping her pickle spoon. The cupboard door swings open. This tremor seems far longer than usual. The noise of the shaking is more unnerving than the movement itself.

It stops.

For several minutes Linda stands staring at what she can see of her apartment in case it all starts moving again.

She picks up the salt-shaker and closes the cupboard door.

Someone knocks on the door.

'Did you feel it?' Linda says to Misa, opening the door.

'No. What?' Misa's all pink from the cold, unwinding himself out of his long scarf and trying to read Linda's Christmas cards on the bureau.

'The tremor.'

'Really? I didn't notice anything. I was walking. It's windy, so everything was moving anyway.'

'There's been so many lately . . . Scared me to death,' Linda says.

Misa is bending over to take his shoes off. 'Oh, you've had your hair cut again,' Linda says. He self-consciously smiles and pats down the top of his hair 'Mm . . . last week.' Linda laughs. Misa hates to have his appearance drawn attention to.

Gesturing him to sit in the apartment's one armchair, a comfortable cane thing, Linda warns him not to follow her into the kitchen. 'I haven't done the dishes for a week – You stay there. What would you like? One sugar isn't it? – In your coffee. Or do you want green tea?'

'Coffee thanks.'

While Linda makes coffee Misa looks around at her livingroom. It's not as expensively appointed as Nicky's is. Foreigners like Linda and Nicky can make, for an hour's English teaching, up to six times what Misa can earn for an hour's washing up in the snack bar he works in part-time. But unlike the Nickies who run after the every Yen teaching, getting their adored Caucasian faces on television and their bodies onto magazine fashion pages, Linda does not exploit such opportunities. She has put herself (as much as possible as a foreigner) outside the syndrome of the Misas of Japan paying for the Nickies to parade before them spouting the Imperialists' tongue and possessing and wearing the appearances the Misas are led to believe they would so dearly like to have.

'Like an Arnott's biscuit?' says Linda coming from the kitchen.

'A what?' Misa takes the coffee and milk jug from Linda's hands and puts them down on the table. 'An Australian biscuit,' says Linda squatting down on her cushion by the table. She jumps up again almost immediately to turn the cassette over in the player. Misa marvels at her restlessness. Drinking his coffee he is amused at the way Linda is now sitting cross-legged, mannishly, like an Indian. How different from Japanese girls, he thinks, who sit demurely, legs folded neatly and elegantly shut to one side like a fan. But that's Linda; he likes her for being different.

Linda and Misa drink their coffee and talk about New Year's Eve plans for tomorrow. 'Don't worry, it's only made of milk and arrowroot,' she says when she sees Misa warily regarding his Arnott's biscuit. He takes a bite. Just then Linda can feel another tremor, a slight one. She ignores it, lest she be thought a panicky foreigner – 'I'm going to the temple tomorrow afternoon with Harriet and the others. To pay the New Year respects. Nothing Buddhist though. You want to come too?'

'Yeah,' Misa says, taking some tablets.

'You alright?'

'I've just had this awful headache all day. I'm okay.'

Thinking about New Year's Eve now Linda wonders how Tatsuo might spend it this year. She got a Christmas card from him two days ago. She misses him.

'Oh, I almost forgot,' she says, suddenly getting up. 'I've got something I want to show you.' At her bedroom door she says, 'You know how Kenzo wrote music. Well the other day Kenzo's mother sent me back some of my books Kenzo borrowed a long time ago. I'd forgotten about them. In one book I found some papers – notes and music – ' Linda disappears for a second. She comes back out of her room with the notepapers.

'I can't read the Chinese characters. Can you translate?' Misa takes the papers and tries to read the random scribblings Kenzo made – 'The music moves around and around on its axis. It is a sunflower turning with the sun. It has roots going deeper and deeper into the desert for moisture. The music is now black, then grey, then white, then clear. I hold that clarity before me and focus through it as I must see through to the stars on the other side . . ' Then there is where Kenzo copied out some bars of music from the Choral Symphony and from 'If I were a Carpenter', and some words from Schiller's 'Ode to Joy', as well as his own words, which Misa reads: 'If this Song of Joy is true, then . . If I can be true, then . . . ' – that's all, there is nothing more to be read, and Misa stops, and falls into a puzzled silence.

Linda thinks to herself – 'Now black, then grey, then white, then clear' – What funny things to write. What does it mean? She feels it means something to her. But what? She looks at Misa. He has put the sheets on his lap, and is staring at them. He looks up and says, 'He was so strangely serious about everything.'

'How do you mean?'

'Just everything. He was always so . . .' Misa falls silent again, then says with increasing agitation, 'Like – You know how he, he didn't tell me but I found out by accident, how he was doing voluntary work helping to build a work-skill-learning institute for the disabled in Koto-ku. And you know what else he did one time? I met him. He locked his door and wouldn't let me out. He'd given me a little antique Buddhist effigy. Incredibly valuable. I didn't know if he was joking or not. I got a bit frightened when he wouldn't let me out for a while. We arranged to meet again anyway but I didn't show up. It would've been the fourth time in ten days. I've never told you but I was sitting in a coffee shop watching him across the street waiting for me. I just sat there and sat there and got more and more scared and didn't know why I was scared or couldn't move. But I couldn't cross the street to meet him. After half an hour when he finally left, I nearly ran out to stop him but I knew that if I'd done that I would've felt forced to tell him where I was waiting and how I felt. Then I knew I would've gotten involved with him in some horrible way, too deeply. That's the trouble with people like him – they flatter you with the way they get you in, but you're put off at the same time. In some ways he was repulsive – sex all the time. I mean it just went on and on and on and I couldn't stop myself because I knew he wanted every inch of me, I'm not saying I'm anything special he just wanted sex, but he wanted all of me so much I couldn't help myself.' Misa breaks off, red in the face. Linda has never heard him talk like that before. She's almost gaping at him. His face is an excited confusion of embarrassment and annoyance. His voice now becomes lowered and muffled and he speaks to the arm of the chair as if looking at Linda might stop him – 'I used to know when he was watching me. He thought I was asleep. I pretended to be asleep. I couldn't bear the stupid terrible way he was looking at me. As if he pitied or loved me or something, as if he was going to kill me. That's what I think. I could've been the one he killed. What would you have done? Can you blame me for just sitting there and not going across the street? I would've killed him first. That's what. I don't know why he wanted to kill anybody. There was something good about him all back to front coming out the wrong way. He couldn't help himself . . .

'I don't know what I'm saying. My head hurts like hell – ' Misa reaches for some tablets. 'I think I'm going to be sick – ' He lurches off to the toilet.

Linda stands there, bitterly regretting she brought Kenzo's papers out in the first place.

When Misa comes back a couple of minutes later he sinks down and crouches on the floor, ball-like, covering his face as if trying to protect every inch of his body. He can't squeeze tightly enough into himself. The sight of this creature without its shell, as crushable as a snail, horrifies Linda.

She puts her arms around him and, rocking him back and forth, comforts him, the mere act of consoling someone else consoling herself also. Misa is brought back from his grief and is restored to himself and he is more glad of Linda now than he has ever been of anyone.

Linda is now lying on her back on her own futon, her hair in a pony-tail thrown over the pillow. She looks over at Misa – now, sleeping quietly on the spare futon. His little face, under the hill of quilt, looks much more peaceful now. He couldn't possibly have gone home tonight, Linda says to herself, giving her pony-tail a flick. How strange that he got all worked up like that, she thinks again. I've never seen him like that before. He seemed so reserved and unemotional . . . She nods off to sleep for a moment. Then wakes up again . . . She was again seeing herself lying in Kenzo's arms in this bed, as lovers. The thought's too painful and useless; she rolls over and pushes it all out of her mind.

But then something else comes back – Black then grey then white then clear – the words made a morse tapping on some hard covering in her mind. Linda wearily resigns herself to poring over the words, setting them this way then that, and running through them until she's convinced they mean nothing. She feels doomed to a sleepless night. She waits . . . ten minutes pass . . . a degree of increase of merciful drowsiness . . . verging towards sleep, thoughts talk mumblingly and idiotically among themselves, talking one another to sleep . . If only I had my old Buddhism back . . happy set answers, step-by-step solutions to enlightenment . . . Roll the ball down the lane and even if you don't knock them all down first try you've got your second chance . . . a second chance . . . Karma . . . a next life . . . No – No, thank you – No more set formulas and textbooks, have to find out by myself . . mumblingly and idiotically rolling over the grassy hill down to soft deep grassy valley sleep . . . If only I could die now I'd be perfectly happy . . . Life's a bummer . . . If only I could die now slip off in sleep I could face up to whatever is in store after . . . What? – No, I don't want to die yet. Only want to sleep, to sleep, to sleep deeply and wanderingly, and softly and slowly . . . The white the clear she drifts off, alone in her boat, carried by the current not by the wind, her eyes turning up sightless like a caryatid's, weary of staring so hard for a coastline.

In the middle of the night Linda woke. The dark room was ticking quietly as if inside a large soft clock. Something was stirring. Linda had the powerful sensation an angel was there in the dark. It was trying to communicate with her, put thoughts in her head. The day she was sitting in the coffee shop the angel had materialised as a Nō mask in the rose design of the coffee cup she was staring at. No other way to try to communicate with her then because her doubts about Buddhism and religion in general during and after her north Japan trip were still effectively repelling any direct contacts by any supernatural beings . . .

Linda blinked in the dark, and became more awake. What was this fantastic thing she was thinking? She couldn't believe it.

But then she stared and listened again.

The angel in the dark was wanting to communicate its chagrin, its regret. After Kenzo's death this young and inexperienced angel had realised there had been better ways to leave Kenzo than through causing his death – it could have turned itself into carbon dioxide and passed out of Kenzo as an expelled breath, or even by becoming something Kenzo would forget and without thinking expel from his mind, such as a train-time he had to remember for only fifteeen minutes or so. While it was in Kenzo's body the angel thought it could leave Kenzo by music, by intensifying Kenzo's desire to create something out of himself; that proved impossible because Kenzo had made the music so completely his whole self the music blocked all exits. It had also occurred to the angel that it could have left Kenzo by semen, but only when the orgasming body is totally self-forgetful and undistracted is that possible, and Kenzo never reached that intensity which could have allowed an angel to leave his body.

Linda's sudden feeling of sexual embarrassment at the thought of Kenzo's semen stopped the communication (or flow of her own thought, she didn't know which).

But then the sense of something in the dark communicating grew strong again, and she heard – Kenzo was headed, in his desperate quest for emotional release and freedom from his past and future, towards some kind of violence anyway. The angel, like an escapee, only took advantage of the first way out and struggled through, felling anyone in the way, the boy Kuni. However the angel now knew there were so many other better things it could have done, or brought about – it could've even somehow directly communicated to Kenzo that it was inside him, asked for his cooperation and left him in a way perhaps even beneficial to both. But for the hapless inexperience of youth.

So now the angel was here with something specific to convey to Linda. But what was it? What was it?

The angel was now moving about the room, restlessly. Misa stirred in his sleep. The angel stooped down and assumed breath-like hands to softly caress Misa's brow. It pitied Misa. It was true what Misa had said (the angel had been listening) – He could've been the one Kenzo killed, was driven to kill. And it was with Misa that Kenzo nearly released the angel through a nearly self-forgetful orgasm . . . The angel moved away from Misa and became immaterial again. It regarded the curled-up Linda for a moment as it prepared to will itself away.

It would be back.

Linda lay still for a moment, then started sobbing.

She wakes up. A tremendous surprise. Disappointed at waking and being expected to climb back onto her horse in the merry-go-round. She clutches up through the air waking clambering out of bed, the rubber band in her pony-tail messed and pulling her hair. She jerks it out with one hand, the other hand fishing about for her dressing-gown. Casting looks at the slumbering Misa boy in the grey light. Then she stops. Quiet. Something is different. It is too quiet. The room seems wrapped in a huge quilt. Dulled no sound. Linda crawls suspiciously, hopefully, a possible rising thrill in her breast, to the paper shoji windows.

Slips it open an inch, then thrown back a yard. The great discovery . . . The garden, the world is covered with snow. The long night has brought down deep snow to fold and envelope the world into itself. Linda takes a long delicious breath . . . Springs through the window driving a cloud of white breath before her into the pristine garden in the surreal glory of snow. Snow. The trees, the bushes, the cars, the fields roofed over with snow. She skips and bulldozes and stomples through the garden yelling and laughing. Churns it with her feet into whipped cream, shakes down the softest castor sugar from the pine branches. The world is pure, untouched, ecstatic for an instant. Rubbish and nonsense about angels evaporate – She knows it – Her inability to accept Kenzo's death creating angels in her head – I'm not mad. I'm sane. I was dreaming.

She crouches like an animal sniffing. What is it? What is the good scent coming through the air, the clipped, the cutting diamond air?

The freezing through her bedsocks. A plop of white topples off a tree and lands on her shoulder. She shrieks. She falls back and throws open the bedroom shoji even further and . . . Making a snowball tosses it in at the warm and grub-soft Misa. He leaps awake, aghast. He can't believe it. Linda climbs back in to drag him rubbing the sleep out of his eyes into the garden. Though he's woozy and outraged Linda's infectious exhilaration gets him. They romp like bear cubs just born hurling snowballs, soaked to the skin, berserk, memoryless, in pyjamas. The first feet in the snow. Their laughter brings the neighbours to their balconies and their children squeal and tug their fathers' pyjama cords.

Now they stop. Still. There is a red camellia bush under through snow. Red arc. White arc. Brown petal edge. White flowers burning. They watch it entranced gazing for a long time. It is beautiful. It is true. It is there. They are there. Everything is together in itself where it is. They are together peaceful.

Now it is afternoon. They straggle up the lane, heels sinking in snow, flanked by ceramic-white fields, the knobs of old cabbages peeping through here and there. The dead cabbage smell emanating even through snow.

The afternoon is leaning past three o'clock. Blue sky filtering through grey cloud then swiftly, a wind having risen, cloud sliding back blue sunlight striking off every snow crystal. They are crackling through meringue-crust snow. Slim green bamboo is leaning over heavy with snow. The snow splits underfoot.

Harriet screams. Her new lover Yoshida looks up. Linda and Misa turn around. Harriet has wobbled her ankle. The pot-hole escaped. 'Are you alright?' The lover asks putting his arm around Harriet's. 'Yes wonderful,' she laughs up, every pot-hole cavity in her teeth glistening in the sucked-down sunlight.

She marches ahead to lead the way. She alone knows this short cut to the temple where they're going to help ring the bell at midnight tonight it being New Year's Eve. A bell to be struck 108 times.

Linda turns to Misa and touches his arm, 'Will you be alright? . . . Your parents really don't mind your being out on New Year's Eve do they?' Misa says they don't mind but he knows they really do – judging from the tone in his mother's voice when he rang this afternoon. But still, it's not every day you get the chance to tramp through snow to ring a bell. A great, thick, bronze bell which will echo through the night under the slow impacts of a carved log.

Aah the blue sky is now clean and absolute before all eyes. It overrides with brilliant indifference aspersions on telephones and guilt at not being at home. And fabulous Harriet is in charge, handing out raisin chocolate to be gorged upon. The chocolate was bought in a little shop in the village by the sea where the bus stopped. A sea brushing the hair back pitting the snow on the shingles with salt. The strangled and twisted seaweed. A half-frozen sparkling jewellery from the village shop window gilt and brocaded girls in kimonos could be seen swaying and tripping forwards like ostriches to the shrine. They were overtaken by the two foreigners and two Japanese. The crowd stepped aside for Harriet to present herself at the shrine's front to ring the high bell on the rope and clap her hands to call down a god to protect her in the coming year as the others prayed to the same god to protect them from Harriet.

Few of the people there appreciated Harriet's reading aloud in Japanese to all and sundry the board inscripted with the shrine's history which they could have read for themselves anyway. Misa was embarrassed on behalf of the Japanese present. But, as she is the boss of today her showing off is not to be questioned. She must lead the way and Japanese love leaders when they can find them.

Down a side lane now. They stop to admire an outdoor stone nursery. In Japan stones are as important as, if not more than, flowers and shrubs in a garden, so they are collected and sold as connoisseurs' items, graded into the green, the dark, the veined and the huge. Each stone here is draped with its own ermine stole of snow. Behind them are pine trees whose branches are supported by bamboo trusses and ropes against the loaded snow. For the same purpose, the trees are corseted in straw wrappings. On the spot Harriet gives a lecture on Japanese gardening explaining how trees and stones are treated as if they were human because they might have spirits in them. Though interesting she is hard to move on. Wary gardeners are now creeping out like beetles brandishing straw broom claws. Linda nudges Harriet along.

They climb closer towards the sky. The snow is drastic against it. In its turn the oblong of a bare black peach tree orchard is contrasted by the snow. There is nothing blurred or indecisive about this landscape. Linda is relishing the clarity and brilliance of it, despairing of her memory's inadequacy to retain it. So like that snow of the Japan Alps it will soon be gone, melted, becoming obscure and humanised again. The sun which elucidates this pristine scene is the sun that will destroy it. Even now the sun is turning it to water, the drips creaking and whispering like a kind of phosphorescent insect-devouring something which cannot be seen. Every second spent in this landscape is vital, irretrievable, agonisingly fragile. So Linda hoards the vision of it, secreting every tone, line and plane of it into herself where at least it may live a little longer.

The group turns another corner, each of the four having felt, in his or her own way, an increase of poignancy to the brink of unbearability in themselves the feeling which made them turn their backs respectfully on the etched fields and the rows of distant fir trees the abstract magnificence of which will soon fall apart and be dissolved. Never could it all be so clear again. Not a doubt could exist in that snow landscape. But doubts are there, to the side, shadows stealing forth slowly across the whiteness. At least, Linda thinks, it'll be sunset soon and the darkness of night will hide the dissolution which I don't want to see taking place.

Having turned away, the scene already becoming a memory, they come to a stand of camellia trees. An old barbed-wire fence prevents them from going right up to the trees but the fallen scarlet petals on the stark snow can be bent down to and touched. By only Harriet. Linda shrinks into herself. The petals, as if still possessing some warmth have burnt holes for themselves in the snow. Embedded, they are sinking. The random yet inexplicably calculated pattern of the red and white shifts across Linda's eyes. She can't look away. Spellbound by Harriet's sacrilege. Linda suddenly wishes someone would stand near her. But they are far away.

She sees Misa pick up some snow and examine it. He too seems sad. She hears Harriet accost him with her rehearsed joke and accent Ar ya gunna see the Empra the day afta tomorra at the palis?

Linda could almost feel the snow cringe.

The snow. Retreating back. The sunset. The night now. The side of a cup tapped with a spoon. Warming drinks for everyone at the temple. Reunions, but no sad memories. The end of an old year. The tap of a Buddhist ring against a ceremonial saké cup. It rings. Custom and ritual to absolve the past. It rings. Louder and louder through the torch-lit night, as down the great temple roof the snow gradually slides. It drips. Heavy off the eaves it falls. Down the eaves below it slides again. Drips and falls. Finally to the soil of the garden where it vanishes, having passed into another form of water, having

gone the way all life goes . . .

Forever forever it seems, a ring a booming hollow ring echoing the night until it shudders. It is New Year's midnight. The great log lifts back in its rope sling to descend, horizontal pendulum, on the carved bronze flank of the temple bell. 108 strokes. The group takes turns. Kenzo's father the priest, his younger brothers and Harriet, Yoshida, Misa and Linda. A shiver goes up Linda's spine as she pushes her body against the end of the log as if the log were this new year launching against the bell of resolution and hope. Everyone is jubilant, strong, making clouds of white in front of their mouths. Snow is falling again – A reprieve, a benediction. Linda rejoices and sweats under her jumper. She is glad of the great night swaying bell. She is crying. With hope.

3 | Outside Kinokuniya bookstore in Shinjuku. Tatsuo grabbed her from behind so the chance to worry about if any ice was going to have to be broken was grabbed from her before she'd even had a chance to worry. His grin had never been more crookedly saucy, his way of holding himself never more a challenge, yet a macho pose, yet an invitation, yet a rebuffal all at once. Just how she remembered him from long ago. He even kissed her, and she kissed him back staggering about laughing through the tinkling January ice on the ground.

'Well you're back. And late!' She started talking nineteen to the dozen.

They talked their way down the street, Tatsuo giving his account of his extended stay in Silicon Valley. The Americans had finally gotten sick of him and with warm courtesy encouraged him to go back to Japan.

They talked their way into a Pizza Palace. Linda ate her way through her excitability until she got quieter, noticed Tatsuo actually wasn't talking as much as she'd thought he'd been, pushed the remnants of her pizza to one side, and asked him – 'How's your apartment after Ricky left it?'

'Still in one piece. Not having a bath in it is inconvenient. I wouldn't mind a bigger place. You'll have to come over soon when I've got the place fixed up a bit. The housework's a bore.'

'Yeah, it gets tedious after a while. All that. Every day – You get up in the morning, get dressed, go to work, come home, and that's all. The everyday routine, like a wall – too high to climb over, too deep to dig under, too thick to push over. . . (New Year resolutions never last long!)'

'I thought your Zen takes care of that problem?' In America Tatsuo had become passingly interested in the Zen of his own country through the influence of his American friends. (Quite a place that California: Zen, Disneyland, AIDS.)

'It's supposed to. I've tried it, and everything – The temples, meditation, even a bit of Zen archery – I'm a bit sick of Japan I think . .'

Tatsuo laughed, 'Don't forget I'm Japanese.'

'No – I'm not sick of it. It's just that I feel I'm going in circles. Achieving nothing. I don't know what's wrong with me. Where am I now? I can't stay in Japan teaching forever. I've got to go back to Sydney one day. Then what'll I do? I don't know.'

'Take your Zen with you.'

Linda said, suddenly irritated, 'After a while all these Buddhisms and Christianities and what have you annoy me. All these set recipes to enlightenment or salvation. Then people get so put off when they don't work. It never occurs to people that they've only themselves to blame, they never stop to work through their own problems . . .'

True enough, Tatsuo thought, also thinking Linda was still the well-intentioned lightweight intellectually, but not quite as superficial as she used to be. But so a lightweight? Diamonds are pretty light too, he thought, and said half-teasing and grinning, 'You know what they're doing, are going to do with computers?'

'What?'

'Have computers with electrodes attached to brains and programme to induce Zen states. Same effect as your meditations which take years. Then they'll have one day some super-advanced microcomputer planted directly in the skull and programmed to create the any desired mental state without your having to have the years of practice to develop the will-power you need to create the desired mental state. All the present computer technology is outside the body. One day it'll be all inside, augmenting the brain and linking to some central information terminal. You know – Those big *Star Wars*-style TV games you sit inside. Well one day some central computer terminal will play the game directly into your head. . .'

So, Linda thought, Tatsuo's eyes have been dazzled by the baubles of Silicon Valley. And have his other attitudes changed too? 'The way you put it it sounds like enlightenment and TV games are and will be the same thing.'

'I knew you'd say that. You've got me all wrong. I'm only warning you about what could happen to your Zen once somebody links it up with your personal computer.'

'. . Sounds pretty cheap.'

A shudder came up through the chairs and table legs.

'Did you feel that?' Linda twitched her cigarette like a pointer.

'No what?'

'Wait. Feel it. A tremor.'

Tatsuo's and Linda's glasses of water clinked together by themselves as if toasting each other, the ice-cubes rocking ponderously like little icebergs. Only the people seated perhaps noticed the movement; the waiter walked over it obliviously.

'Yeah I can feel it.' Tatsuo said. They sat there poised as seismograph needles. Linda looked about the restaurant. The fish in the aquarium were swimming the same as before. Only the light shades hanging on their long cords from the ceiling made the slightest edging to the right and to the left. The restaurant, swathed in the building, was being rocked as gently as a cradle, the legendary snake under Japan stirring in its sleep.

'Nearly gone now,' Linda said, blowing out a stream of smoke. 'We seem to have been having a lot of tremors lately. They're funny aren't they. You can't even trust the earth in Japan. In Australia the sky moves but hardly ever the earth. It's the weirdest thing when what's over your head and under your feet move at the same time. . .'

The tremor had returned, sharply then vertically. The plate-glass windows banged in their frames. Cutlery near the edges of tables shivered off onto the floor. A tray of plates fell off the servery counter and a woman sitting nearby yelled as her leg was splashed with miso soup. The building jerked as though a ship grinding onto a reef. Several teenage girls were uttering little whimpers and heading towards the door, but then, at the door, as the tremor passed, they were marooned in a moment of terrible, giggly indecision before finally prompting one another to return to their table.

Linda and Tatsuo looked at each other.

A waiter turned on a transistor radio and Linda could hear the news-flash that the Kanto area had been hit by a magnitude 4.4 tremor.

Linda said, trying to sound calm and understating and Japanese about the whole thing, 'That was a bad one.' Quakes were the last things she wanted to think about. 'Think we're in for a big one? There's been talk.'

Tatsuo smiled at her indulgently, 'I wouldn't worry about a few tremors. This is Japan, remember.'

She remembered so too. She glanced at a waiter picking forks up from the carpet. Things seemed to be getting back to normal; the woman with the splashed leg was bowing in smiling gratitude for the cloth the head waiter had given her.

Linda said, 'But I feel sorry for the people who have to stay here all their lives. The trouble is though I'm not yet bored enough to want to leave Tokyo and not interested to really stay . . . I like Tokyo, but I don't know what's keeping me here now. There's nothing really. At New Year I thought things were going to get better, but I still feel I'm just waiting around. I don't know what I'm going to do if I go back to Australia though.'

She saw that the waiter had put the tray of silver back on the servery counter.

'Yeah,' Tatsuo said, 'a lot of foreigners come to Japan all enthusiastic and don't know how long they'll be here. Then they finish up staying here for years and forget why they came. It gets to the point they get into such a groove here they can't muster up the energy to leave even if they want to.'

'I know. I don't want to see my hair greying in Japan but then again I don't want to see it getting grey in Australia either.'

'Who does? Some people seem to think they can stay in suspended animation in Japan and not get old. Then one day they're forty and it hits them they're out of the running if they go back to their own country.'

'Oh come on! Let's shut up,' Linda said, gathering up her bag. 'Let's not get all gloomy the first time I've seen you back. Look, there's a party on tonight. Come and see everybody. . .'

That night Linda dragged Tatsuo to the party and, already having gotten herself half-drunk at home, enthusiastically introduced him to Chris and Misa and Reg and the others. (At times a certain part of Linda's mind seemed to have no taste buds about the combinations of people she so eagerly tried to salad-toss together.)

The next day however, when she met Tatsuo again for lunch, she had an obscurely ominous feeling she wasn't sure was her hangover or something else.

Cooler today, somehow edged and calculating, Tatsuo lounged back in his seat regarding her.

'How did you like the party?' Linda asked, hoping her bleariness would excuse her.

'Mm. Fun. Funny how you got to meet that Misa,' Tatsuo said casually.

'Oh Nicky knows everyone at that disco you all go to.'

'Do we?'

'Oh Misa does.'

'Your pet wombat?'

Linda looked at him with a weary smile. She thought – What issue are we dodging? And didn't know herself. And dodged off in a different, but maybe really the same direction. 'What do you think of Harriet after all this time? She's talking about getting married to Yoshida now. She seems pretty well set up. Maybe I should get married to a Japanese. I don't know if I want to give them what they want though – You know – The little Japanese wife act – staying at home, keeping the dinner hot, serving tea and slippers, sex once a week. I want my own life, a career. I like teaching. At least that's something. But things seemed clearer back before. . .'

'Go on.' Tatsuo was sitting slumped and comfortable with his arm along the back of the long wall seat. But there was however, a steady accretion of surface tension, as of near-transparent separate layerings of lacquer becoming blacker, one under the other. Until you could see your face in it, anything reflected, but less and less visible from within.

'I mean um. . . Isn't it awful how people go away. No matter how much in love you might be with a person you're always basically alone. I envy artists and priests. The priests have their Buddha or Jesus to love. Jesus and the Buddha don't go away, if you love them. And the artists have their pictures and music – True, those things aren't so permanent either but they're more permanent than just love. Sometimes I really wish I had the one strong talent, or abstract devotion, something to save me from love for another person.'

'So who's this person you love?'

'Oh I don't mean anybody now. . .' Her eyes were now wandering about the room. She couldn't look at Tatsuo, whose stare was now absolutely level, withholding, and chill; the pupils burning.

The look then passed away so completely and quickly and abruptly Linda couldn't even remember he'd looked like that at her. Suddenly thrusting himself forward and taking a long sip of coffee he then said, 'Be back in a minute. Gotta make a phone-call. Remind me to ask you about filing cabinets when I get back.'

'Sure.'

She watched him cross the room, and felt bothered, and stirred up, and puzzled and confused and everything. With the spoon she patted down the sugar in the bowl. Her emotions became a bit calmer, damped down. She stared peacefully at the soft white sugar.

Then it happened.

She started to feel that ominous, different stillness grow rapidly within herself. She felt the talking in the restaurant become light and distant. Some switch seems to be quietly thrown and she feels herself sitting in some other room. The angel is standing there, looking at her. She listens with stricken obedience. The angel wants to apologise to her for Kenzo's death, atone itself. But how? Bring Kenzo back to life? It can't do that because it is beyond the angel's powers to bring the dead back to life, and the fate of Kenzo's spirit is equally a matter out of the angel's intervention. Though a super-being it is no perfect being. It can make mistakes and errors of judgement; it is worried now it might somehow blunder giving Linda something just as it blundered getting out of Kenzo. (It now knows how to enter and leave humans with instantaneous ease.)

By gaining its freedom through Kenzo's death the angel has set itself back in its quest for the enlightenment of superbeings. There are no decreed punishments for an angel which causes a human's death: each angel is its own judge or benefactor. So the angel of its own volition has chosen to atone. And it is Linda it has chosen to atone itself to because she is the one who has felt the greatest loss through Kenzo's death.

But so what to give her? The angel wants to know – What does she crave most? The angel doesn't want to give her anything in such a way that she would be either too aware of being given something or totally unaware. She would have to be quietly slipped something she would feel, if she were to be aware of anything at all, were naturally owing to her anyway. . . The angel seems to fade into this problem and Linda finds herself thinking, bewilderedly – But if I know what the angel is up to how can it take me unawares? This question snapped the switch off and she was again sitting in the bright restaurant. And another thing – she thought – How can this angel thing be in doubt as to what I want most if I myself know? – Some kind of revelation or enlightenment or whatever. How can I seriously ask myself what I want as if I don't know what, yet know what I want? Maybe communications with angels (if it was an angel) are so peculiar they can ask you what you want most, know what you want, and yet ask again as if neither party knows what is wanted – Well that's ridiculous, Linda decided, also thinking there was something distressingly egotistical in thinking an angel wanted to give her something.

She had another crazy thought – She knew the angel would be back, but only when it chose, and that she found funny – If it is a creature of my imagination can't I just rub the lamp whenever I choose to, and make it appear? Then again, maybe imaginations don't work quite so conveniently . . . But for God's sake – Angels?! – Is a part of my brain flapping open? Am I mad, or plain stupid? I'll never have any clarity about my life if I continue to be hostess to angels – She thought. Then, suddenly, everything she'd seen, or thought she'd seen, and felt and thought in the last few minutes vanished into a certain kind of amnesia in her mind, and she had no awareness she'd ever stopped staring peacefully at the sugar basin.

Tatsuo slid back across his seat.

'Okay. Filing cabinets,' Linda said brightly.

'Oh yes. You said you had some you didn't want. I need some for all my papers. Can you sell me them?'

'You can have them for nothing.'

'Thanks, that's nice. I don't have a car though – We've got to work out a way to get them over to my place. Do you know someone with a car?'

'Yes.'

'Good. . .' He looked at her steadily and carefully through his long eyelashes. He seemed about to ask her something.

Linda felt the rather deliberate pausing, and tried not to guess too hard at what it could be instead of. She felt driven to change the subject. '. . . So you noticed in America that a lot of people are interested in Zen?'

'Oh yes,' Tatsuo responded eagerly, 'they were making their own tofu and there's all these people in L.A. who make meditation cushions and even tatami mats to put the cushions on – Then they turn around and just use them for theme dinner-parties!'

They went on talking closer together over one cup of coffee after another for another half hour or so, (Linda being struck anew with how Tatsuo could sit and talk about Buddhism and Zen as if Kenzo had never existed – No, Tatsuo hadn't changed a bit, she decided) then the conversation seemed to find itself ironfiling itself back to the attraction of Tatsuo's apartment – 'I'll have to shift a few things around before I can get the cabinets in,' he said. 'The apartment's too small for all the stuff I've got – You haven't seen what it looks like since I've been back. .' He again gave her that look which was both blank and compelling. 'Say, why don't we go back to my place now for a glass of something?'

He's definitely thinking what I've been thinking since yesterday, Linda thought, considering her reply. There was a moment of intrigued suspense, as if she were watching an enlarging penis about to suddenly flip itself free of its bent against whatever was staying it.

Slouched across the seat he was looking at her with a suave little smile, just crude enough to hold her transfixed without repelling her. Which she could've been in an instant.

'Yes sure,' she said, feeling that the moment she'd said that the course before her eyes had straightened out and become smooth and inevitable. That which would, and had once wanted to happen. The Tatsuo of two years ago. The all-night dancing and the Chinese toast. This opportunity to relive. This opportunity to find out if a cave, or further mountains or a sky or a corpse or nothing but ice lay on the other side of that frozen lake in the mountains.

She was lying naked in the warm room, staring up at his shaded ceiling light, tasting on her lips the salt of where he'd kissed her. Touching her nipple she held in her mind the image of his nude back when he'd gone to the bathroom a few moments ago. A little under the influence of wine, she'd forgotten why she had come to be lying naked like this on the bed.

But she was still aware enough of herself to hope it would all happen simply, that she was mistaken in thinking he would need something fancy for him to enjoy himself. It had been so long since she'd last had sex with someone. She could almost hope it would happen so unobtrusively she could easily go back to feeling, afterwards, that she hadn't had sex with anyone for a long time. So she lay there a little tense.

But here was Tatsuo now. He walked across the tatami lightly, lean and relaxed, as if down to some water's edge where he'd quickly crouch down and push himself off on a surfboard.

Linda already felt ready, and she soon invited him into herself so openheartedly she forgot to remember she didn't want to be tense for | 123 at least five minutes.

Tatsuo's fingernails were cool against her shoulders. A spearmint sweetness on his breath. As he came he made no sound but she felt an immensely eased liquidity become her own coming finishing off into soft pins and needles down along her inner thighs.

Then she saw a wordless smile on his lips, all beautiful, nothing at all smug or tight or vain in the corner. And she smiled quietly at the sight of it.

. . Her hand was in the back of his hair now, gently combing her fingers through. His hair was longer than it used to be. She glanced at the two small moles on his neck. He rested the side of his face down on her breast and she could feel the blinking of his eyelashes.

Talking together softly now, she told him about the things that happened while he'd been away, how she'd once had a prowler on her balcony, and about how she's often wished he could've come back, just for a short visit.

Tatsuo looked away. His face seemed to grow harder.

'You regret it now,' Linda softly suggested.

'. . No.'

'No?'

'It's not that.'

'What is it, then?'

He lay on his back, and gazed up at the ceiling. 'It just suddenly felt awful – you and me, and him.'

'Kenzo?'

Tatsuo nodded. He said to the ceiling, 'You and me and him, the three of us too close together, like incest. Having sex.'

She had nothing to say. She supposed so too. Then, just as she felt she was going to get depressed, it occurred to her that this was the first time Tatsuo had ever voluntarily mentioned Kenzo. She lay very still, so as not to distract him. 'Oh I don't think so,' she said, airily. 'It was just you and me as far as I'm concerned. . .' She could sense his struggle to speak, and yet not to speak.

'. . .I think I went a bit funny for a while after he died,' he said, after a moment.

Linda thought: If I touch his arm he'll tell me everything he feels. Hating herself for her feminine tricks she slid her arm down alongside his and quietly began stroking the hair on his forearm. He was still silent. He knew what she was doing? No. He was still staring at the ceiling, and started talking again oblivious of the hand on his arm. He spoke as though slightly tranced; he was watching fascinated the Kenzo in the air, on the ceiling, in his mind, starting to thaw out like the body of someone still alive, frozen for another century. '. .It was pretty awful . . . On the beach after I'd recovered a bit I had to look at his dead body and say to the doctor "He's Kenzo Kuwamoto." Then when the police talked to me I was the one who had to be told "Oh yes, Kenzo Kuwamoto. We'd just gotten the alert to be on the look-out for him. Do you know he was wanted for murder? What exactly was your relationship with him? Did you have any knowledge of any intent to murder?" etc. etc. etc. . .'

Linda knew that side of the story and was impatient and excited to find out what she didn't know. She burst in – 'But how did he die? Did he just drown while pulling you along or whatever, or how?'

Scratching his arm, Tatsuo began answering the question as if it were just something he'd put to himself in the course of his monologue. '. .I didn't tell the coroner this, apparently nobody else saw just what happened, but he sort of went under me. I can't remember how, and he was pushing me up from under . . . I couldn't do much because of the cramp . . .'

'So he actually did something which he would've known would jeopardise himself?'

'More than that it was plain stupid. You don't save a person like that expecting to save yourself too. The whole thing was stupid – him jumping in like that. You know he was a poor swimmer. I was a fool getting drunk and getting a cramp. I went silly. When I met him on the beach in the morning I felt something was funny or different but I didn't say anything. I thought he might've changed his attitude to me. It'd been a long time. I was away too long. Can't even remember now why I went away. So I started showing off to get his attention and drank too much beer. When I was swimming he just sat on the pier looking at me vaguely and distantly . . . To tell the truth when I first felt the pain in my side I was glad because at least it might've gotten the dumb look off his face. This is the worst thing but when he started pulling me along I didn't try to help, I think I even gave him a shove under. You know all the time I was in Okinawa he didn't send me one card. No I know what you're thinking. I didn't drown him. The cramp got too bad for me to do anything but move my legs around a bit. That was the worst part – I was the good swimmer, but I couldn't help myself. And then he doubled under me trying to push me up and – God don't ask me – If only that boat had been a few metres and – God don't ask me – If only that boat had been a few metres closer . . . Can you understand what it is like to feel for the rest of your life . .' Tatsuo sharply turned and glared at Linda. 'Why do you want to know all this?'

Carried away, the amnesia worn off, Linda blurted out, 'Because I have to know if an angel got out of Kenzo by just making him die like in front of a bus or through a self-sacrifice which is the only way an angel could get out of a person when you think about it. . .'

'What?'

'Look I mean, I don't believe it myself, probably he committed suicide, but I've got to tell you –' She gave Tatsuo a jumbled account of her angel visitations but left out the angel's wanting to give her something because she was the one who'd felt the loss of Kenzo the greatest. Horrified embarrassment at what she was saying soon tongue-tied her. She made a stifled nervous sound that sounded like a giggle.

Tatsuo pushed himself up on his elbow and angrily shook her. 'I've never heard so much fucking rubbish –' He gripped the flesh of her shoulder and with his thumbnail digging in he shook her again – 'I'll apologise now so I don't have to do it after but don't you dare talk about him like that – All this angel and fairies crap. That's what killed him. That's what caused all that murdering – all this pink shit Buddhism and trying to find "the meaning of life" and being ethereal about everything. The Kenzo I knew wouldn't have a bar of it. He didn't want to be a priest. It was you and that Harriet bitch with all this fainting around trying to be modern and good and butter wouldn't melt in your mouth that did it –' He smacked her across the face. 'So I've apologised.'

Slumping on his back he fixed his eyes at the opposite wall.

The slap strung but Linda felt unstirred. Lighting a cigarette, she said, 'Thanks for the slap – No, seriously – I needed it. Knock the rubbish out of my head.'

Tatsuo grunted in the dark.

Her head on the pillow Linda looked sideways at the ridge of the cheekbone of Tatsuo's turned-away face. Was he crying? She raised herself on her elbow. No. He was still and calm now. She asked him softly, gamely – for she couldn't help herself, 'Did you love him?'

He said, wearily and stonily, 'Don't ask me, just don't ask me anything more.'

She touched his wrist impulsively. The feel of saturnine stone. His jaw muscles set clenched. Linda wanted to hold him, but she knew he wouldn't appreciate it at all.

So she just lay there, listening to her watch tick.

. . . A tremor came up through the room. Linda sat up alert. It soon passed, leaving the ceiling light swinging leisurely on its cord. 'That's the third since yesterday . . . Don't they scare you, after a while?' she said.

'. . . Yes,' he replied, looking at her at last, 'a bit.'

And she looked at the swaying light again and felt she'd rather look at that than into his eyes where the other side of anything had never stopped retreating back.

A week later, Linda was sitting on a tightly upholstered sofa realising she was sitting in the middle of a faintly absurd long frilly dress she'd put on thinking it was feminine. One hand was clutching a half-eaten taco and the other itself. Tatsuo was standing over her, looking tough and tired, manly and pitiable all at once, slouched on one hip. He handed Linda the letter and said, 'You better have this. I found it crumpled up in his desk drawer. He meant it for you, it's dated the day before he died. I've been keeping it all along, I'm sorry, and I've read it. I think I must have been jealous of you all along.'

Linda read it quickly:

I don't know why I'm writing this. But I have to communicate with you. You're the only person I feel I can open up to. I couldn't have wished for a better friend.

I don't mean to sound like this, but I feel something bad is going to happen. Do insane people know if they're going crazy? I can't be a priest and I can't not be a priest. I want to live outwards and fully but maybe I've misinterpreted my whole life up until now. Can you believe how difficult it is to break out of a pattern of living you've been in since birth? I was born in that temple. The smell of the candles there and that wood, that old dark polished wood, it's still in me.

What a confused note to write you. I don't think I can give it to you. But listen, remember this, I've always loved you as my dearest and only friend.

– Kenzo.

After she'd finished reading it she distractedly pretended to reread it to give herself time to think of what to say to Tatsuo. He seemed to be expecting her to say something significant, or even apologetic. So she sat there looking down at her faintly absurd frilled-up dress, feeling like a paper rose in water, expanding and expanding and loosening and the air all around like water going pink. But she had nothing to say at all: there was little in the letter she didn't already know, except Kenzo's avowal of love, which, when she'd read it, made her feel so alarmed and persecuted in front of Tatsuo she wasn't sure if she'd read it or only imagined she'd read it.

'. . . Well, thanks,' she finally said, looking up. Tatsuo shrugged as if it now meant nothing to him. And left the room with one of his bruised-up masculine movements he was not altogether unaware of. All smokey but hard and sudden. She felt a still-hard cock had been pulled out of her somehow sideways. All hurt and seeing itself by surprise in a mirror. Everyone surprised and off-angle, all this business between men and women and men again. This sex intruding on Kenzo's letter. Which she pushed sideways to the end of her knee so she couldn't make out the writing. But then that was all. There were less and less reactions. The more she didn't know if she were Linda or the tightly upholstered chair or the dress or the taco coming back toward her mouth or the letter or whatever person it was who was supposed to have been Kenzo's dearest friend.

The following Wednesday at the school she taught in Linda was informed she'd been dropped from the new programme. It was explained to her that the school had come to the decision that two female speakers of Australian English (her and Harriet) were one too many for one school, and since Linda had been the shorter time at the school she was the one who had to go, unfortunately.

To her surprise Linda discovered she felt almost nothing about being fired.

(But, she thinks, the power of the vision of the thing – not the optical illusion physicality of it, but the strength of the feeling of the angel's presence, would almost make me believe it were real, if I was sure I wasn't going mad and headed for the psychiatrist's couch, or if I were to stop telling myself there are no such things as angels. . . . Really, I don't know what to think anymore. I know I am not mad, but I know I'm not 'sane'. So what is it, Linda, my friend? Tell me.)

Evening. Misa at home in the kitchen. Family arrangement still life group portrait. Father, Mother, Grandmother and Son. Each to their function. All held in composition by the television. Positions starting from the left – Father, chortling silently at the antics of the spangled and microphoned idols on the screen, peeling himself a tangerine. The shells of thick skin by a cup of green tea, the leaves settled on the bottom, darting a little like fish when the cup is lifted. A little pot belly under the father's grey-green cardigan. An eye to the Son an eye to Mother next who moves her hands with abstracted celerity among sliced onion, cubed carrot and apple pieces. She is composed of gathered shadow, painted against the sink and cutting-board. Various points of light – the orange of the carrot, the brown of her eyes and the pinks of her nails, she is not sepia-coloured. Unfolding herself, one petal at a time, she creates dinner.

Son receives the apple from her hands. There is a toothpick in each peeled section. They are eaten with a few quick strokes by the calm and sturdy son. Son of the Earth in beige pullover. Legs planted apart. A cake grandiose in front of him. Hovering yet obdurate on the fringe of the suspended animation is Grandmother, permanent in her chair, no wave being able to reach her now. Her threadbare laughter trickles out at the antics on the TV. Father makes a traditional and time-worn joke about everyone on the blue screen looking like pumpkins to him. Another laugh leaks out of Grandmother who is killing time for her tea to go cold. That's how she likes it. A programme appears on the TV about the '23 quake – The narrator voices the current speculation about another big quake. And interviews some steel-rimmed expert who says the Kanto area's seismic tension has been exhausted for hundreds of years. But the next guest-speaker warns that covered well water-levels on Izu peninsula are rising. Grandma holds up her foot to display the '23 quake by the burn scar on her heal. She chortles and lets her tea get even colder. Father reminds everyone of the popular theory that big quakes occur every sixty-nine years. Mother accidently steps on the gas tube and is puffed at by Father. Talking about the 1920s what was life like then? Grandma knows all about it as she plots in the back of her mind the complex manoeuvres for getting to the toilet. Nobody notices her body language now as the Moscow Circus has come on TV, so she is not helped to get up. Mother's back is turned aquatically shadowed hands in the water onions rising to the surface. Nothing rising except a burp out of Father nothing at all rising in Son. Son whose hand by its determined movements no matter how small can make primal territory out of the table top, cups, sugar and specs all encompassed within reach. To attract attention Grandmother stirs her tea and taps the side of the cup with her spoon. And Misa notices nothing, nothing, only longing to go to the privacy of his bed.

Tonight in his bed alone Tatsuo cannot get to sleep. He is tingling with a nameless excitement. His mind will not slow down. The cold air is like rubbed silver. Unable to find anything to centre his excitement on, Tatsuo is merely relishing just lying under the blankets with the edges of the cold air burning near his face. If he were more sober he wouldn't be able to find anything to be so exhilarated about in the past few weeks. One pick-up after another flicking past monotonously like cats' eyes in the road. Spending his money faster than he earns it. Only glad that he and Linda could stop having sex without losing the friendship. Making himself sexually temporary again was the only recourse against fears of singularity and old age and death and everything unavoidably specific. For you find yourself in a corner when you paint the floor mortal the way he does. Usually. For tonight is just a bit different. Maybe because of thinking of the relief of getting that Kenzo letter off his chest. Nothing in itself but it meant something to Linda. A relief she could have the freedom of knowing. So now he doesn't mind so very much. He can pass his hand over his soft things in pyjama and not feel the shiver of flesh which craves to be touched and persuaded it is immortal.

A spark now flies from the increased friction of his excitement shooting along the cold night and illuminates a vast, usually dark space in which he sees kindling and doused fires, the increase and decrease of the body's lustre, the extending and withering of ferns, the wax and wane of summer and winter – the growth and decay of all things – at least for the duration of that rocket's exploding and lighting up the whole sky Tatsuo has been freed from and rejoicing in mortality, clearly understanding that this very detached joy itself will pass away soon to sink and become strata in the layers of his memory. The memory of all existence. The memory of the earth rejoicing so freely. So free to move in any direction now Tatsuo is glad only to be still and relish in his possibilities, to lie still and be gradually replaced by sleep. Tomorrow he will be the same as he was yesterday but tonight, just now, he has been different, the possibility having increased that he may continue to be different again one day. Tonight he can sleep knowing that he is an optical illusion of molecules looking at one another sideways, that he is something in name only, that everything he does is predestined to become nothing. Tonight he can sleep replenished in that knowledge, a crest of cold air by his brow.

It is very late. Alone in his bed Misa is one-dimensional, illuminated by only one front light after having moved forward from a rare shadow of self-obscurity. A conjurer's hand has to move above and below Misa to prove there are no strings. He is controlled by subtler things than that. He can fool many, the many who may not believe he is pure and simple through and through. Everything he does and thinks is as clear as a well-cut slab. Things end at Misa. Porous, he absorbs all, little goes through him. He leads to nothing. But he is imaginable. Concrete, yet a cut-out from very fine paper. He stays easily in the mind of a friend or a lover as does the shape of a geo-metrical building or a symmetrical mountain. He stays in the mind. Alone in bed tonight Misa is thinking about Nicky whom he loves as much as one-dimensional, photo-of-concrete slab love can. Nicky likes him but of course doesn't love him. Nicky never does. Misa knows that and could almost become embittered by it. Misa is so likeable, good-natured and moral he is rendered almost unlovable to all but the Kenzos of the world. Somebody's ideal, somebody's unattainability. That's how it should be. In themselves Kenzo and Misa's moments together were perfection.

Thus Misa now thinks about Kenzo. Misa is an old-fashioned photographer who takes long quiet daguerreotypes of people for his memory. Portraits with plenty of space between the frame and the face. Misa is afflicted by the thought that no matter how lovingly we mount and frame our portraits of our friends, they invariably one day begin losing their original colors, crack and curl up. Nothing can reverse the process once the portrait is done. So little survives. All is lost and forgotten. The stars we clutch at dissolve in our hands. The hand that clutches dissolves in the air. The air. The sky. Nothing is consummated once and for all though that is what we think we want. The only things approaching anything near permanency are our frustrations themselves.

Misa curls up deeper into his quilts, withering in the cold night, likely to, in a cold dream, be blown and blasted away to dissolve eventually into the cold minerals of some infinitely distant planet. The pulse of warmth that holds him to his warm bed is as weak as the ligament that attaches him to life is frail. As frail as anyone's. Disappointment finally soothes Misa to sleep with a silent prayer that the world will not change too much again too quickly. In sleep he is very much alone in a bed on this earth tonight.

It is true. It is too late. Harriet dribbled ink on her new page before she could get the Kleenex to the nib. Now the page is spoiled. She crumples it up and throws it away. After that little interruption Harriet must now tune tight again the thin stinging strings of her mind. She then tests them out with the note of a Zen word and sends it vibrating tapering off along the chosen string until it resonates in space. It seems to work. Harriet cocks her head, pen poised, as if listening for the sound of the resonance of her own mind. She is satisfied. It resonates away into nothing.

All is now quiet and calm. All Harriet's lines are still, separate, gathered only where she moves her pen. There is the scratch of pen on paper but otherwise all the clockwork and revolving stages and turning books around her are still. The more her being focuses sharpened into the tip of her pen the more she is pared down to nothing, exquisite nothing, all surplus cut away, mechanicalised, ritualised; Harriet sits at her desk writing about brain-waves, the brain-wave patterns of Zen.

She puts down her pen again. And chews a fingernail. The density of brain waves inside her has spawned a thing which is worming and eating its way out of her, towards the light, towards anything high and blue and sunny. Towards Linda, the object of Harriet's female jealousy, the forming object of Harriet's perverse love, (a love however, which all the same thought nothing of quietly lubricating the engineering of Linda's dismissal from her job; matters of survival and keeping a roof over your head being, as always, the first priority.) Well perhaps Harriet loves Linda now simply because Linda, being Linda, lives a differently shaped existence from Harriet's and therefore, by decree of Harriet's tribunals, must be incorporated into the Crown Lands; or maybe because her cut and dried life needs a little Linda moisture to soften the leather; or maybe even simply because Linda is a woman and will leave fewer bits to be spat out after being consumed. Fortunately for Linda, Linda is unaware of being on the way to being loved by Harriet.

However, this circuit of Harriet's of unconsciously devising ways of making Linda acknowledge and love her only in order to then pitilessly toss her to one side is really just mortal game, a respite from Harriet's Promethean labours with Buddhism.

So Harriet now turns back to her desk, as natural in relation to the desk as is a rudder at right angles to the back of a boat. She takes up her stylus again to mark a new white page. Here now, the pitting of reference against reference and scholar against scholar is the true battleground of Harriet's life. All else is play. In this battle, pitched in libraries, in tutorials and on research grant application forms, from no matter where Harriet may be tossed she always lands on the four feet which will spring her back, yet again.

But, she too must rest, take stock. Alone at home tonight, in her hothouse study, she is sitting with her feet in water, hoping her head will bloom like a flower in enlightenment. The waiting for Enlightenment. The arms race for the ultimate weapon. Enlightenment – it's like the extra bit of sherbet her school friend got which Harriet didn't and thus was so jealous she could have crippled her little plaited friend. Harriet's part in the Race for Enlightenment began as the little miss at birthday parties who licked the icing off cakes and artfully arranged them back again on the plate.

But everything that hinders our pursuit of Enlightenment must be tossed overboard so now she could almost cry aloud with impatience Oh Why must we eat, excrete, and fuck at all? Her body tonight, with its occasionally emptying stomach and filling bladder, seems to Harriet like a great useless suitcase to be lugged through the crowded air terminal of busy Zen terminology and paid exorbitant Customs for. The price one has to pay for the body. If only she could be just a brain in a glass container of chemicals attended to by lab assistants and left in peace to do its thinking. If only, if only she sighs . . . The room suddenly jerks, jerks as if it were a vehicle bumping into the back of a car in front. The driver was not paying attention, thinking about something else . . . The tremor passes. Harriet's heart is however still beating so quickly she thinks crossly – But how can you always be ready for a blasted tremor? She should be – A true Zen preparedness would not find its heart racing so quickly just because of an earth tremor.

And that indeed makes her think about her Buddhism again. It has often worried and tested Harriet that what she is after – Enlightenment – unlike a concrete goal like a certain sum of money to be saved for, is by its very nature unknowable and indivisible. She has come to believe, without telling herself too insistently that she believes so, that the academic cutlery is the only way by which you can get at and divide the problem of enlightenment. That way, she knows in her heart is second best, but there is no other way for a person such as Harriet who cannot accept the fact that she has acknowledged emotionally something which is too elusive for her intellect to tolerate.

What she essentially wants is a technique, (Zen being one of its names) a method which could secure for her, via the necessary power over herself, power over the every last square inch of the world when and where it comes into contact with her, a method which would satisfy any situational or passing moral and social requirements without satisfying them unnecessarily, yet a method which would not ultimately call upon her to disclose or justify how she had obtained the measure of power she might by x-time have secured, for she believes that the method itself, by the stringency of its academic or other demands upon her, is already in itself her just punishment.

What Harriet and Linda want of 'enlightenment' (for want of a better word) is not different: power over things external via power over things internal, but what they want the power for is different;

Harriet as a person is already pulled together as closely as a string purse, but Linda . . . Harriet's concentration falters, the pen droops between her fingers. Some accursed dampness is getting into her thoughts and is softly undermining them. Is it old age? She's barely thirty. Is it Yoshida sneaking into her mind without a ticket? Harriet snaps off the main light and returns to the area of her desk lamp in which she is enclosed by circular, globular night. There is nothing out there except the cold night. But Harriet doesn't mind the cold. No Zenness indulges herself with heaters . . .

Harriet's mind is gently caving in, a tissue in water, sleepy. That's it. She's sleepy. She should go to bed. At that realisation her pen stiffens again alert in her fingers. In control again she tightens up a few pegs on the pegbox of her mind. The damp of nothing retreats again beyond her circle of light. She is again a pioneer, the unknown gnawing and cringing back, hissing and enraged but thwarted only for the time being. Its prey will keep. Harriet squints at the light bulb. She looks at it curiously. It has her in thrall. Harriet is an insect now. The dark out there, she is crawling around and around inside the light shade, trapped, blinded by the very light she greeds for, refusing to go to bed tonight.

Sitting on her meditation cushion Linda makes her spine as straight as possible, tucks in her chin and sways to the right and left in preparation for meditation. She hates herself for having dragged out the old meditation cushion but she felt impelled. She couldn't escape.

As soon as her breathing becomes light and regular the initial chaos begins. A gold Buddha as large as a star suspended in space appears cradling in its lap the dead Christ. Increasing in size blotting out everything a pig runs up a tree among thousands on a cliff in a canyon rich with autumn colours. The pig gives birth to another pig in the tree then eats it. The pig throws itself over the cliff, falls, but never reaches the bottom. It vanishes to be replaced by a leaf falling upwards which finally comes to rest as a gilded leaf in a crown.

Linda sees various martyrdoms. St Catherine on the Wheel crying out as a set of silver and glass revolving doors turn as the universe emerges as a drop at the end of a syringe in an experiment. A red and black Coca Cola sign grows in intensity. Men and women in a space station slowly circling Pluto dine off quail and lamb by candlelight. Linda is invited to join them. Pigs and people trample up the stairs of a tower to rooms where saints are sleeping swathed in their long golden hair. The Buddha takes Christ down from the Cross. Down a hill runs Kenzo clutching his brown robes. The pigs and people butt in the doors and the saints dash their heads against the walls rather then be done to death by the animals. The universe, disguised as the universe, passes through the glittering revolving doors. Men and woman set down their knives and forks and listen. The galaxy creaks. The dish runs away with the spoon and the little dog laughs and Kenzo was going inside out. Before and after history with a shove in the back each from the Buddha beautiful youths and maidens swing down by the million on long silver ropes through the universe. It becomes a legend a myth a mass a beatific ecstasy. The mountains have never risen more sharply and the skies have never been more sapphire. A sieve in the air. A computer card in the universe. Linda can see through to the gap on the shelves of the circular library where her life should be. It has been taken away from the place where universes are as small as full stops becoming molecules in the air separating for an instant as the chant can be heard. An angel flies into Kenzo and is trapped and makes him die to escape because Linda's pride of friendship doesn't want to imagine Kenzo as a plain murderer who couldn't ultimately control himself. Then she drowns as Tatsuo in Kenzo's arms her lips on his. The white loin-clothed gods enter the frozen sea with white papers between their lips and drag the entangled lovers' bodies back to the pure snow beach. Where they become rotting octopi prodded by the curious angels one of which becomes a real angel of all things and hands her enlightenment on a plate in return for having taken Kenzo away. Then the real angel disguised as that angel reveals itself and says This is the only way I can communicate with you – through the confusion of your meditation. You are mistaken in thinking you have dreamed me up because you cannot imagine Kenzo as a murderer; I exist, regardless of everything but myself. True illumination, your gift, is now nearly yours to take. You will obtain the purity and resolution you crave. You are at the perilously momentary brink from which you can take it. One more leap of your mind and . . . The little dog laughs and something runs away with the secret. The universe rings with the taunts and secrets of a million silver creatures swinging across it. A giant frog croaks like the Buddha. Men and women and children and saints and martyrs take up their knives and forks again. And turn away. Everything dies. There is nothing left. A car roars past the room. The images then spin so fast they blur transparent, then white, then grey, then are black. Linda's spine sags and her breath comes in gasps. The sky rises and rises into the hurricane until it is a dot disappearing. Another car roars past the room. The clock can be heard ticking . . .

Linda stirs. Wide-eyed staring at the wall which reveals nothing.

5 The next afternoon, Misa was driving Linda over to Tatsuo's with the filing cabinets Tatsuo wanted. According to the car radio, the temperature was six degrees celsius, with a strong northerly wind blowing down from a high pressure system over eastern Siberia.

What funny information, Linda thought, hardly able to think at all today, after her poor sleep last night. She felt drained and hazy. Yet she continued listening to the news as if it were important.

'Do we turn here?' Misa asked.

'Yes. Straight left.'

They were driving through Shinjuku. In the afternoon sun the clustered Shinjuku skyscrapers were pale blue and green, laminated silver. From the car turning the corner they appeared to revolve, the thousands of silver windows like solar panels pointing the sunlight at one curve. Far down below in the plaza, the light solemnly slipped and see-sawed along the aluminium wings of the giant kinetic sculpture. There was a steady march of people, back, and forth, across the brown brick plaza. And up again, beyond, could be seen on the tops of ever-newer skyscrapers, the gaunt cranes lifting the city into the sky.

The car was now nudging its way with the traffic over the bridge over Shinjuku station. Towards the bridge was approaching a train heading towards the city centre, its 'Tokyo' destination panel the epitome of efficient expectancy. In the stopping and starting car you could hear the crisply slinging sound of the pantographs just before they were muffled under the concrete.

On the other side of the bridge the car turned past some neoned ice-cube of a building. Then there was a dark brown ship's funnel-shaped thing with no windows, but everything in it, according to the illuminated directory, from Hawaiian restaurants to health studios.

What funny buildings, Linda considered, everything striking her today as unamusingly funny, vacuous and idiotic. She felt completely insubstantial, only needing the window to be wound down a crack for her to escape as surely as cigarette smoke. She doubted her sanity; she doubted everything.

She looked about for different substance. There on the steering wheel were Misa's neat little hands in their white mitten driving gloves. Making a turn this way then that, his hands were steady and certain. Why on earth though he was wearing mittens on a flannel-sheathed wheel Linda couldn't fathom. Maybe he just wanted to be sure about everything too?

Looking out the window she thought of Tatsuo. She vaguely hoped he wouldn't be too condescending with Misa. It had been very good of Misa to offer to drive the filing cabinets over. He was always sweet. But what did his sweet little brain really think about?

Gazing out the window Linda saw a girl selling flowers on the foot-path, and Linda wanted to know what she thought about too. Then she discovered she was in fact wondering about what she herself thought about, as if she truly didn't know. Her thoughts this afternoon couldn't have been much more diffuse. She tried to get them into some kind of nutshell, and asked herself again, (over and above the question of angels and sanity and delusions) – How do you really make your spiritual beliefs and values work, in the everyday, outside of temples and churches? How do you do everything, while trying to be reasonably good, in the everyday of your life? What Kenzo wanted to know too.

She thought she knew how to in theory, but not in practice. Though there was something right about the question, the way she put it to herself was wrong, she suddenly felt, just as quickly feeling a cantankerous distaste for setting the problem as a 'Religious' problem. Her thoughts were muddled again. Staring at the car radio she tried to refocus – The act of unlocking the problem, she felt, was some unimaginable trick of not using a key to it but being the key yourself which in the turning becomes the exquisite room you want to open and the dark one you want to step out of – In short – No A then B then C steps of separate procedure but an act which is A, B, and C all together as one letter, which is also one word you can say as a single syllable, a key sound of all life, its disclosure, its abandon-ment, and its own solution.

She very nearly believed. She believed she now could've been almost capable of performing the unimaginable trick. Perhaps she was now somewhere near the truth of her life, that which would realise it. A needle eye existed to be pierced by a thread end, but the place she was in was dark, her concentration poor; she would miss the silver eye as does virtually everyone, all the odds stacked against her. To miss the silver eye by a centimetre is no better than missing it by a metre. There are no prizes for well-intentioned errors. She was now both the twenty-six year old Linda and any seventy-six year old Linda: any Linda in fifty years time would have no greater chance than she had now. So near and yet so far; her moment of near salvation and clarity was becoming the moment of being carried away by the perverse rip currents within herself. And so she faded away unto herself again, despairing, yet too tired to know just how much she was despairing, her thoughts breaking up into the changes of the passing scenery. She was sitting within the hum of a car as the hum of the car, and there she remained, indistinguishable from anything, until they arrived at Tatsuo's, where she'd forgotten everything, again.

All diagonal smiles, Tatsuo came out to greet them. He kissed Linda on the cheek. 'Met any interesting angels lately?'

'No.' She ruefully smiled back. And felt her mood lift.

They all then set to work getting the filing cabinets out of the back seat of the car. They carried them inside and started helping Tatsuo rearrange the furniture.

Every so often, faint, but short sharp vibrations were coming up through the room. 'Feels like the lid of a rice cooker coming on the boil,' Linda said, nervously ready to laugh about earthquakes if anyone else did. There'd been those shiverings since morning, every hour or so it seemed. Tatsuo muttered something and continued grappling with the bookcase. His face was pale and set. Easily unsettled today, Linda felt a moment of panic – she suddenly felt alienated from Tatsuo and Misa, imagining them now assuming some fanatically stoic Japanese preparation for the worst. The moment quickly passed, as it should have, for the only thing Tatsuo and Misa were feeling fanatically stoic about at the moment was trying not to sneeze on the dust while lifting the heavy bookcase away from the wall.

'Why have you got to rearrange the whole room?' Linda asked querulously.

Tatsuo put down a pile of books. 'It's so cramped in here there's no other way to fit the cabinets in . .' He wiped his forehead. 'Oh I just remembered – Harriet asked me to ask you to go over and see her tonight.'

'I better go over and see what she wants then' – Linda felt glad of the opportunity to go and see a Western person, any Westerner. But she didn't like her desire to run away. 'Can I leave you two to it?' she asked shyly.

'We're right here,' Tatsuo said.

'I might come back later on, but I think I'll probably go home afterwards.'

'Thanks for your help,' Tatsuo said, putting a drawer of a filing cabinet back in.

She ran through the cold night air feeling thoroughly unhappy.

Harriet let Linda in throught the main front door. 'Chris is here too,' she said.

'Tatsuo said you wanted to see me about something.'

'Yes. Come through . . .'

They went into Harriet's study room. Harriet picked up a large folio book from the desk – *The Buddhist Treasures of Nara*. 'I got it for you. I've already got a copy but I found this on discount in one of those little old Kanda bookstores near the British Council Library. I thought you might like it.'

Linda was no more interested in the Buddhist treasures of Nara now than they probably were in her, but she was touched – Here was Harriet trying to be nice. As awkwardly as any usually self-possessed person is when not fully realising how ridiculous she's looking bending over backwards to undo a wrong. Linda knew it was Harriet's background bitchery that got her dropped from the school: Linda had a secretary friend there who'd been watching Harriet's machinations all along – For one thing at a teachers' meeting which Linda was foolish enough to miss, Harriet subtly managed to draw attention to how many meetings Linda had missed, the same meetings which Harriet had dutifully attended.

But Linda now accepted the book, and felt nothing, not even a desire to take Harriet to task.

Harriet could hardly look her in the face. And found some papers that needed realigning on the other side of the desk.

Actually Linda was preoccupied by something else now – There was a Buddhist angel in the cover design of the book. It had never occurred to her that her angel was of any particular religion; it was just a woozy madness appearing everywhere, and here it was again, sending its brother or its sister to torment her from a book cover. She felt so cornered she wanted to lie down on the carpet and surrender, but whatever it was she'd surrender she had no idea. She just badly wished the angel would go away and never come back.

Chris called from the livingroom.

Harriet called back, interrupted in the middle of checking a page of footnotes, 'What is it?'

'Bring Linda in here.'

Linda put the book down on the desk and went out. As she went down the hall she could feel a kick-jolt go through the house. She stood at the livingroom door – 'Shit!'

From the sofa Chris said, 'Well I've got my earthquake-kit bag packed. But tell you what's worse, what I wanted to tell you – Heard about the crack-down on cultural visas?'

Coming into the room Harriet said, 'There's a scare every year. I wouldn't believe it.'

'But this time they're really weeding out the people working without permission on cultural visas. And that means all of us.'

'Where did you hear it?' Linda asked.

'A friend of mine. He got caught.'

Sinking down onto the end of the sofa Linda lit a cigarette.

She felt cold-stomached. Her visa renewal time was near. She vaguely supposed she would go home and vaguely type up her visa application making up a story about how she supported herself. She worked herself into a mental knot trying to decide just how much money she had in the bank – $2,000, or $2,100'?

Harriet dumped herself in the large armchair and said, 'It's only a scare. Forget about it . . .' She patted the arm rest. 'Who's for coffee?'

'I don't know,' Linda said.

'You'll have one Chris?'

The lamp behind Harriet was making a silhouette of her latest hairdo, a festive battlement. 'Stay the night. We can play scrabble.'

That did it – Linda stood up – When you played scrabble with Harriet she stopwatched everyone and didn't let you eat your biscuit during your turn. 'Actually I think I'd have more chance of getting my visa than winning one of your scrabble games,' Linda laughed.

Chris hooted with laughter at Harriet. Even Harriet giggled, in that
142 | teeth-bared implosive way of hers. And Linda felt better – Because

we laughed there isn't going to be a visa crack-down – she told herself, remembering her childhood superstition that if she jumped into bed from the chair, and only the chair, the crocodile under the bed couldn't snap at her ankles.

Getting ready to leave she threw the scarf over her shoulder. She was worried there'd be nothing to laugh about before she got to the door.

'You're right!' Chris boomed, jumping up, 'If you get caught you get caught. And if you don't, you don't. And Bob's your uncle!'

As Linda rewound her scarf around her neck she observed Harriet suppressing an urge to ask her again to stay the night, an urge indeed to flounce and thump her stick like Betsy Trotwood.

'You live down my line don't you?' Chris said to Linda, 'We might as well go together.'

After seeing them off, Harriet came back into the livingroom enjoying after all the prospect of a night by herself. Yoshida was away in Hokkaido skiing. Thoughts of visa scares diminished in proportion to the rising anticipation of the little dish of chocolates she'd take to nibble when she started work on her latest paper on Buddhism.

Walking to the station Linda asked Chris the time. '8.40,' he said.

'The roads still seem busy,' she said, also wondering at the sight of someone down the street moving house at this hour of the day.

'Don't laugh but I've got a job for you,' Chris suddenly said, 'They need a teacher at this school in Ochanomizu . . . '

'Yeah?'

Tatsuo and Misa have gotten hot and dusty from shifting the furniture around and getting the room back in order. Misa offered to stay to help Tatsuo. Blandly and parasitically sweet, Tatsuo thinks. Misa means nothing to him, just some friend of Linda's hanging around. But Tatsuo wonders what is really watching from behind that rather dopey little face. He is sure Misa is ascribing to him all sorts of complex and sissy emotions concerning Kenzo.

Throwing a jacket over the back of a chair Tatsuo wants to laugh. He feels like giving this Misa Teddy bear a prod to see what might happen. Or is he just another cock that thinks it is a person?

As Misa dusts about with a pan and brush Tatsuo yawns. Like Linda he is feeling rather washed-out today, after last night's mental excitement. As he foresaw, his fine thoughts in bed last night are finding it hard to survive into this next day. Such being the ups and downs of coming to grips with anything.

'Say,' he says, swinging on his swivel chair, 'what do you think of this flu going around lately? Think we're heading for an epidemic?'

Misa shakes his head gravely and tries to answer the question seriously.

Tatsuo laughs, and bounces off the chair. 'Look, I'm all dusty. I'm going up to the public bath-house. You coming too?'

Tatsuo throws him a towel and a bath bucket. And wants to laugh and say something crude – like, 'Is your cock as wrinkled and worried-looking as your face is?'

But he doesn't.

Outside the apartment Tatsuo beats his chest and whoops and breaks into a jog.

Misa runs to catch up with him. When he comes alongside Tatsuo gives him a laughing shove – 'You're alright,' he says. 'I'm not going to bite you. Thanks for helping out.'

Then he turns away and yawns again and walks slowly. Feeling as dark and impregnable and self-hating as he thinks Misa thinks he is.

Linda and Chris are standing in the first carriage of the Chuo line express, leaning on the rail behind the driver's compartment. From here they can see the track ahead. This spot in the front carriage is popular with passengers who like to be able to watch the silver rails shoot under the driver's window. It helps to alleviate the long hours of daily commuting. Tonight, the train being not so crowded, Chris and Linda have the window to themselves.

The train has just come through Koenji station and is rolling almost noiselessly down the gradient in the elevated track. The next station – Asagaya – Chris's – can be seen in the distance. A yellow Sobu line train in that station is closing its automatic doors in preparation for leaving. Linda watches it with her usual train-lover's interest. Gathering speed on the descent, her own train is shooting above the roof tops and crowds of late-night shoppers.

Looking away from the widow, Chris thinks of something else about the teaching job, 'They want someone who can teach mornings too.'

'From what time?'

'Usually from ten.'

'So I don't have to get up so early?'

'Don't be lazy.'

'I'm not!'

'You are.'

'. . . Wait . . . Something – ' Linda cocks her hand.

The train is jolting. Linda glances down at the driver whose hands are tightening on the brake. The train seems to be leaping and bucking forward. A murmur goes through the carriage as heads turn. But no one seems especially alarmed. The train is slowing down, the jolting rapidly becoming more violent and vertical. The Sobu train, on the approaching descent, is also pulling up. Clutching Chris's arm Linda sees gaps appearing in the distant side wall of the elevated track.

– She is now lying on top of Chris in a corner of the sixty degree angle carriage, her fingers in his mouth. Bags hair glass umbrellas Chris's fright-fart. A slithering kick shrieking derailing the spine of the train broken to a halt the Sobu train in the opposite direction going over an upending concrete section sending ten yellow carriages trustingly following the rails into an ignited block of shopping and running below. Bars and shops mushroom-cloud leaping up into sparking pantographs tearing down walls of tipping concrete Linda's head hitting a chrome pole as Chris wrenches her loose of their own train leaping with gravel and elbows and fingers onto whatever had landed first on the gravel and elbows and faces beneath.

Tatsuo drops his clothes basket. Misa picks it up for him. The sound of a semitrailer passing on the busy road outside the public bath-house prevents Tatsuo from hearing what Misa has just said to him. Misa, already undressed, going through the glass doors to the bathroom doesn't repeat what he said.

Tatsuo unzips his jeans quickly and takes them off with his briefs |

at the same time so they'll be easier to get back into later. He shoves them into a basket and reaches up to put the basket on the top shelf alongside Misa's.

At the sliding doors Tatsuo can see that the wading-pool-sized bath is already fairly crowded. The steamy air is thick with the smell of soap and chlorine. He spots Misa sitting on a low plastic stool, starting to wash his hair in front of the long low wall mirror.

Tatsuo drags over a stool and sits at the set of taps beside Misa.

'It's hot in here,' Misa says, lathering his hair.

'Better than cold.' Tatsuo is looking at himself in the mirror, wondering if he needs a shave.

'I wonder what the time is . . I have to be home by ten,' Misa says.

'How come?' Tatsuo glances at Misa's body. Misa seems made out of rounded compact things like apples or potatoes. Is that what his appeal was?

'My mother wants me to take over the counter in the snack-bar.'

Pushing the soap down his leg, Tatsuo sees Misa looking at him in the low mirror. The smoothness of the soap makes Tatsuo feel even sleeker. He lathers himself displayingly, but not exhibitionistically, just enough to distract Misa. 'You still live with your parents?' he asks, with a slight teasing sneer.

'. . . Yes.' Misa is throwing buckets of warm water over his head and shoulders.

Tatsuo starts shaving in the steamed-up mirror. Misa now goes over to the side of the bath. By the time Tatsuo finishes Misa is stretched out soaking in the simmering water. This is the best part of the bath ritual. His head is resting on his folded towel on the edge. Lazily scratching his pubic hair, he lets his arms and legs float drowsily upward and outwards.

Just as Tatsuo is crossing over to the bath the wet floor goes to the right and then to the left with one pure and absolute movement. The counter-crack cracks the ceiling. Everyone looks up blinded. They are sluggish in the hot bath. A part of the ceiling comes loose a ceiling beam coming down hitting the side of the bath in a splash of splinters. The floor throws Tatsuo back onto his feet aiming his eyes at the door where he goes in all directions at once cracking bath water flooding him perversely where he wants to go but after a thousand moments the memory of Misa. Stopped still a milli-second on the wave-breaking floor. Fuck the cunt. Hauling back down-

stream negotiating what are now tile-edged rocks arms and legs sliding pink water steam shrieking the cursing cracking floor. In a frenzy Misa's leg handfuls of ankles and wood the side wall balloons inwards a truck appears the driver's face a matchhead in a wind bathers up around the wheels like new red tyres. All arms and legs Tatsuo hauling Misa through the shattered glass doorway a pounce of flame behind them up the petrol river leaping onto the backs of whoever are stuck last through the door.

Linda and Chris are clutching each other picking their way down the elevated track. The train is behind them now, bright orange whenever the sky-hurling flames on both sides of the elevated tracks leap on one anothers' summits to get through where the sky used to be. There's not much room for everyone – on one side half the elevated track has disappeared. On the other – a thirty-foot drop where the side wall was. Everyone is inching along, stumbling, ants on a high-wire, crying and tripping, stunned wordless. Only inching along. Linda's teeth chattering into Chris's shoulder.

When she feels the thrust again she doesn't feel it because nothing has stopped moving to her but all of a sudden the movement makes a big space under the feet of two people stumbling along. A concrete drop. Nine pairs of hands grabbing at anything in the opposite direction. Go like roped mountain climbers over the edge. An animal shriek Chris goes too Linda's shoulder bag in his hands Linda lying flat on her back on a rail in the opposite direction.

She lies there, curiously spellbound and quiet. When she gets to her feet she doesn't even remember who Chris was. She doesn't know who the people are who are getting to their feet around her. It's raining. Linda looks up and hopes it'll rain. Then she remembers it's raining and she better shut the windows. Then she remembers there aren't any windows. Why aren't there any windows? She forgets to ask someone if everything has stopped. She gapes instead – from this height, a panorama – A city on the surface of the sun. There are branches of fire, waving and thrusting into space, sometimes doubling the heights of the buildings they are consuming. Out there there are chemical storage plants and oil refineries burning metal white. Tokyo Bay covered in burning oil. Tidal waves rising, carrying swells of burning oil and ships on their sides over the roofs of Koto-ku, Haneda and Kawasaki.

She jerks awake. Ash is being blown off her face as fast as it hits it. From the top of the heat updraft into the sky debris is beginning to topple back down. Large as walls. The booming and roaring in her ears she drags the scarf around her head and stumbles forward.

She reaches where the Sobu train went off the tracks. Being the lowest part of the elevated way this is the only place she can climb down – sleepered rails hanging down ladder-like. A yellow carriage underneath. She crouches down and takes hold of the cold rail. It shakes. Chunks of concrete to the street below in a smack of white dust. Thrown back on ber bottom she vomits with fright. Wiping her chin with her scarf she sobs confusedly and wonders why she's sitting in a couch. Why do I want to climb down? Where to go? All directions. Stay here. Until the fire catches up. Safe here.

Rigid.

But two moments later she is climbing down the broken steel ladder, a dazed monkey. Where is Tatsuo and Harriet? Eight minutes later she discovers she's standing on a fallen concrete block near the bottom of the tracks. A throng is trampling back and forth. In front. Surging into the traffic intersection. Massing inwards as bees keeping the young cool in the centre. A woman in a slip can't get in. A blackened sexless crying. The crowd. Swaying.

Now getting hotter, going around and around, swirling, people grabbing at reinforcement rods jutting from Linda's block of concrete the children becoming imprinted messes of wool on the floor of the crowd. Nobody hears them in the new roaring of fireballs scooped by the wind off the tops of buildings hurling over the intersection Linda throwing herself down the manes of fire flying over. The back of her hair frizzing up in flame. The scarf smothering around her head she loses her grip and rolls backwards across the concrete in the same moment a water tank on the top of the building opposite explodes down through the neon signwork grilles. Fire water and glass flooding across the sky Linda going rolling down the slab coming to wedge in the space of another block the crowd going under the upside-down river.

Harriet has gone around her cracked but still-roofed house snapping off gas valves and catching in buckets the water left in the taps. 148 Osaka-Radio's blaring. She is now in the garden throwing buckets of dirt at her burning plum trees and washing while beating sparks with a blanket. Then the smoke and wind-driven heat get too severe. She goes back inside and wets a blanket and lies on the floor under it. And expects the house to explode in flame at any moment. It doesn't. The wind changes direction, pulling the fire-storm elsewhere.

Crouching. A puddle of blood. Four naked nearly dead people. Under the fallen front awning of the bath-house. Tatsuo crouching over Misa in a puddle of blood spreading to the curb. Cars exploding and twisting in the street. People tripping, scurrying, ducking hubcaps and doors. Doors like back to front shields flying in the wrong direction. An oil shower burning on the awning. Tatsuo trying to push Misa's feet into the boots he grabbed on the way out of the bath-house at the same time pulling sandshoes onto his own feet cut. Bleeding leg and shoulder burns Misa swooning. Onto his back Tatsuo drags him from under the burning awning. A few seconds staggering along the street then a look back at the bodies jerking into life screams – red, a few seconds, the awning down-crunched. Lurching in one direction his head can't turn back around – He can hardly take it. That you can die like that. A reflex burn chilling through his own body, he lugs Misa along cursing. Misa is sobbing with pain. Tatsuo hits him in the face. With a shock he sees he is naked. Deadweight. Slippery with blood. Tatsuo discovers himself as naked as red too. But no pain. Where are clothes? Piggy-backing the dead-weight down the concrete soon a fur boutique. All funny, still standing. Plastic-glass showroom window in one piece on the footpath. Misa is dropped like a kitten out of a cat's jaws onto that. Protecting his soft things with a cup hand Tatsuo leaps through the window attacking a dummy. A fur coat, then another. Tatsuo follows the furs in a leap back through grabbing display cloth on the way. Crouching on the plastic he feeds Misa's red arms into the slippery cold sleeves. Binding Misa's thigh. Himself into a fur too.

Just then people at the back of the shop. Ransacking drawers and shelves, arms loading with ermine and sable. They see the blackened figures on the footpath. See nothing. Turning back to pulling and stuffing with faces of desperate and terrified enjoyment.

Tatsuo blinks at them. They are looters but so is he. One of them the old lady who runs the tobacconists next to the bath-house. But not important, surely now. Gas-main lids across the street are shooting out like champagne corks. Jets of flaming gas into the sky.

Misa baggage a side of pork on his shoulders again. Mustn't stop. Terror his nerves will never be able to remember to avoid and yet get to objects all at once. That garden. Harriet's. His face a white wall. A sphincter opening and closing in his head. Sheer terror begins he mustn't stop must be what he is becoming an animal ferocious hunting the prey which is safety for if you're not possessed to insanity with a refusal to die a rage to live you will die from now on between this street and that garden gravity reversed roofs sucked straight into the sky in the heat updraft three people charred together straight up the sky chimney Tatsuo would've gone too with Misa had he not barnacled the fire hydrant until the feeling of his shoulders dislocating nearly became the disassociation He wouldn't he wouldn't the refusal to let Misa flood away when the hydrant burst its neck pinning Misa to a wall breaking a rib than let him go the crates the nails sticking out Hydra's heads somehow he knew when to stumble just when to duck the Sony sign the tile rain through the dropping TV antenna cage somehow he did it.

In Harriet's garden melted coat hair your own face eyebrowless shoes cut through to bone slumping on brown winter grass on their backs in a faint. Chest heaving. On his back staring stupidly at the silent Misa. Staring stupidly at his own silence through Misa. The beginning of numbness. His throat moves a bit, swallowing. His eyes shut. And passes out.

Linda is treading over a long and narrow thing. To get to the next main street she has to pass through this alley between two buildings. Packed down together are a few dozen corpses. Soft flagstones. They have not been burnt to death but compressed by a down-draught of scorching air while they were trying to escape from one street to the next.

When Linda reaches the next street she opens her mouth.

She only retches as there is nothing left in her stomach. She leans against the wall with the intention of sliding down and going to sleep or dying. She is black, bruised, half her hair frizzed into hundreds of tiny bubbles, the stench of which makes her mouth open again.

And that makes her lip bleed. How and when she put her tooth through her lip she doesn't know. And how she ever got to be here she doesn't know either.

She leans there hardly breathing. Someone comes up from the side and punches her in the leg.

'Get her out!'

Linda turns. There is a four- or five-year-old boy whose face is streaked with dirt and tears. His little red mouth is pinched between his fat cheeks. A pair of gloves on the wrong hands are knitted with the name Haru.

'Get my mother out,' he demands again, hitting Linda's leg and then pulling her by the jeans. She lets herself be tugged over to the edge of a collapsed house which isn't yet burning.

'Get her out.' He starts crying.

Linda can't see anyone to get out. But she walks up and down. Then stops, unsteady. The carriage wall revolves, upwards, the city is a wave, a wall breaking overhead. She puts her hands on her hair and collar. They crackle. The fluorescent light came down. White grains are in her collar. Rubbing her fingers, she discovers ash powder. And suddenly sits down to make the ground stop, going up in the corner.

She retches.

The boy is trying to pull a curtain out from under a beam. 'Get her out!' He is bawling. Getting up, then squatting down again on her haunches in front of the child, Linda starts laughing. Spit from her spluttering giggles gets on the boy's face. He bites her hand. She pulls her hand away and looks at it. She jumps up and runs over to the house ruin. There is no mother but a bud of fire growing in the centre of the wood heap. Turning to Haru who is standing with his back turned to the house, she says, 'Your mother already went out the back way and is looking for you now, over there – Let's go and find her!'

Haru believes the madwoman.

Linda smiles, picks him up and starts walking. Haru starts crying and tries to struggle out of her arms. Linda doesn't put him down. She keeps walking. Haru quietens down. After a while he puts his arms around her neck. She likes that. She keeps walking.

6 The room is quiet, and dark. When Misa comes to, it is to find himself warm, and wrapped in blankets on a futon. His wounded thigh and broken rib and burns are bandaged. He is in pain, but startled more by comfort now, he looks around warily, as if expecting an explanation for his whereabouts.

Also wrapped in blankets is Tatsuo on a futon next to Misa's. Tatsuo woke up a little while ago; his limbs feel more numb than painful. He holds Misa's look and guides it over to the figure in the armchair, the wings of which cast deep shadows around the occupant. Her face is softly lit by the light of a red plastic torch standing on the coffee table. Its light makes a yellow circle on the ceiling. Misa stares up at it. As if he were a baby learning about light, he again looks at Tatsuo for an explanation. Tatsuo's silence is too long. Tears appear in Misa's eyes. Harriet puts her head on one side. She says, in a quiet but alarmingly penetrating voice, 'You'll be alright now.' Misa nods vigorously at her. Tatsuo makes a little smile. Harriet is glad that he has smiled.

She gets up to take the boiling water off the kerosene stove to make hot drinks. She carries the kettle into the kitchen.

About two-and-a-half hours ago, on discovering Tatsuo and Misa in her garden, she tried to get Tatsuo to his feet. Since he couldn't walk because of his cut feet, Harriet had to get him into the house by using the fireman's lift-and-drag technique. It was painfully laborious. She gave herself a strained neck and grazed knees out of it. She was too exhausted to do it again with Misa, so she dragged him into the house on a blanket, thinking at the same time that she should have done the same with Tatsuo. Then, going through her first aid book, she figured out how to bathe and bandage Tatsuo and Misa as best as she could, and fed them antibiotics from a bottle she had left over from a recent ear infection.

Her house, built on solid Yotsuya rock, had not been badly damaged by the quake. After getting up off the floor after the fire-storm had changed direction, she looked through the window – It was then that she spotted Tatsuo and Misa in the back garden. All through the night the comparatively unstunned Harriet knew what she was doing, as always; tonight, the cool presence of mind won from years of Zen meditation had proved a very distinct advantage.

The room is quiet, and dark. Tatsuo's eyes are going slowly around the room. Because of the pain. At the side of the carpet – little piles of swept-up broken glass, pottery and china. Glimmering. In the torch- and stove-lit darkness, things are shadowed beyond the small area of light and warmth. The tacked curtains, when lightly sucked back by the wind, hollow out in the glassless frames.

Near the hearthplace – an Edo-period lamp, with a laquered bamboo base. The heavy wood has a rich, red glow. To its right, is an antique chest, the kind with hanging handles. An embroidered cloth over it . . . The room, even quake-shaken, looks comfortable, and elegant. He feels gradually embarrassed by his gratitude for her having taken him in . . . When he thinks.

The curtain over the glassless window . . .

He feels it – Clenching his teeth.

He shuts his eyes.

Harriet comes back in with a tray of coffee.

The sight of a tray of coffee makes Tatsuo feel oddly intoxicated, revived. Things erased. His right hand and half his left are bandaged, so he takes the coffee mug with difficulty. 'Harriet . . ,' he says, nearly spilling the drink, 'Have you seen my apartment . . ?'

'Yes . . . I saw it out of the front window – It's ruined, but not burnt . . ,' she says gently.

Tatsuo shrugs.

'You can stay here for as long as you like – Misa too – and Linda, when she comes back.' Harriet falls silent, testing the heat of the coffee with her lip.

'Mmm –' Tatsuo stares down into his cup. The curtain sucks lightly in the window. Misa stirs uneasily and painfully on his futon, his eyes following every word.

'What can we do . . ?' Tatsuo murmurs, already realising the futility of his words.

'We can't do a bloody thing. That's what we can do,' Harriet angrily says, hitting the chair leg with the back of her heel. 'She could be dead for all you know – How long does it take for her to get home from here?'

'About twenty-five minutes . . . I don't know exactly.'

'What line did she go by?'

'Chuo, I think . . . You should know. She was here last.' Tatsuo's feet are throbbing.

'Where would she've been at about nine?'

'God I don't know – She might've stopped off to buy a giraffe for all I know.'

'Don't talk rot!' Harriet shouts, 'What station's hers – Ogikubo isn't it? The one after Asagaya. Yes?'

'Yes.'

Harriet's been mentally making the journey back to Linda's.

'I told her to stay here and she wouldn't. She couldn't get away fast enough.'

Tatsuo winces. 'Keep your voice down will you.'

The sound coming out of Harriet's mouth becomes low and vicious, 'I'm going to ring the police. They'll get Linda. I'll ring them now.'

'For fuck's sake calm down. We can't do anything I tell you.' Misa suddenly tries to get off his futon. Harriet rushes at him and over-enthusiastically pins him back down with the blanket thus making him groan with pain – 'Calm down, calm down. You'll be alright.'

Infuriated with his feet, imprisoned in his futon at Harriet's mercy, Tatsuo screams at her, 'Leave him alone you idiot. Stop it will you. Stop it –' He falls silent fighting back tears of exhaustion. Then, sniffing loudly, tries to be calm – 'Please sit down Harriet. Just please . . .'

Harriet, hesitating for a second, then ashamed of herself, blushes, and goes back to her armchair.

Linda is picking her way along a ruined street. A balcony is hanging crooked in the air. All the exposed rooms up in the sky, walls like burnt toast, things hanging on cables, TVs which have nothing to show. It seems that the walls of many buildings just dropped straight down. The heads of some people can be seen up in the exposed rooms. They aren't calling out, just looking down blankly, water and dust trickling down. One building side has a sewage pipe releasing its contents. In the street lettuces from crushed crates have been trampled to slime up the buckled bitumen. A teenager is filling the inside of his guitar with rice from a split sack. Scattering past are dogs with cream on their legs. Near the burst cakeshop window people are trying to move piles of things. But most of the crowd is just wandering about. One young women dragging her dead baby along by the arm.

Linda passes heaps of rubble from under which crushed voices can be heard. She sees a man tugging a woman by the hand from under a beam, but then when she glances back again she realises he is just trying to pull a ring off the woman's finger.

Whenever the ground shivers again Linda sits down with Haru in her arms. The nausea of the carriage. Its length becomes a ship's corridor, going up a wave. She has to sit. She gets down to the ground, before she is struck down. She feels someone trying to lift her by the armpits. Holding Haru tighter she rises the rest of the way by herself, and walks on, away from whoever it was who touched her.

She keeps walking. Tatsuo and Harriet. She starts coughing in the smoke. The smell of gas and sewage is severe. She puts her hand over Haru's crying face. The physical discomfort is as though her coat were on back to front and tightly buttoned.

She is still telling Haru they are looking for his mother. She wants to walk until she falls down from exhaustion, so she won't have to walk anymore.

This street leads into a semi-residential area. By the look of the still-standing smoking house frames it seems this area was destroyed in the fire-storm and not by the quake itself. There are many corpses on the road. Lava casts. Greying in the fine settling of dust.

Linda discovers she is walking through a playground. In the dark she sees many people, family groups. Blankets are thrown around and things are being handed about in some kind of dirty picnic. One or two people in white uniform are trying to orchestrate. Back near some dark bushes Linda has found a swing in a sandpit to rest on. It strikes her as funny to sit here, because the swing frame and the sand are perfectly intact.

After a few moments she hears something coming towards her from behind. Vacating the swing and moving off Linda looks around – An old naked woman in slippers is crawling blind and bleeding into the sandpit. Linda freezes. The old woman suddenly goes small like a spider, coughs, and dies there and then without another movement.

It is very cold. Linda turns away. And continues walking. She makes her way down a street.

When not coughing and sneezing, Haru is very quiet. He doesn't seem to recognise in the dark what might've been the old landmarks of his life. Sometimes his eyes have a hopeful look. Sometimes he rides on Linda's shoulders. As she walks she lets him hold her ear or touch the bubbles of her hair. She is too glad of the child's quiet pre-occupation now to stop him. Slowly, her daze is beginning to wear off.

Some of those half-buried people she supposes she should've helped. But it's impossible. There are too many. And Haru has absorbed all her compassion.

With his soft and warm proximity, Haru is helping to keep her going too. He is something to hold against her cold depression that she is no longer anything she could once have recognised as herself. Living, now, is something which goes no farther than a few minutes into the past or the future. She is an ant carrying a thing bigger than itself, across a fragile diameter of time.

They have reached again the corner she is sure she turned fifteen minutes ago. She's not sure if she's annoyed. There is an abandoned car nearby. Onto the bonnet she eases Haru. Then she sits, and brings him back onto her lap.

Something like gunshots sound in the distance. The shivering of another tremor.

She stares at the ground until it passes . . . Out of the dark, suddenly, a young couple emerges. They stop and ask Linda what she's doing. She's forgotten her Japanese to tell them she's sitting on a car bonnet. They talk between themselves. The girl fishes Linda out some things from her bag – a little map, a pack of tissues. It occurs to Linda that the girl doesn't know exactly what she's doing.

They go away.

Linda looks at the ground again. Haru is dozing off to sleep in her lap now. She draws him further under her opened coat.

In this moment of rest now, on the car bonnet, she feels curiously lightheaded. Then stops thinking.

She looks down. She can't think.

Whoever it had been who got to 9.04 last night, disappeared down 9.04. Only now the fading, after all almost unsurprised exclamation that person threw over the chasm, before vanishing.

That's all.

The front of her unburnt hair is in her eyes. Her eyes are shutting.

The dark cracklings of the night. Slowly, brushing the hair out of Haru's eyes. His eyelashes. Dusky.

Dozing off, sliding her hand across the car bonnet to support herself, she feels something hard and smooth – a pair of false teeth. She lifts them. She lets them click in her hand. Fibres of meat are still between the molars.

Woken by her movement, Haru looks about to start crying. But he sees the teeth, and takes them out of her hand. And tries to put them into his mouth. Linda smiles. Haru throws the teeth away, making a little grin.

Down the street comes running a tall, foreign-looking figure. Something like a shawl is over her head. Her handbag strap is over her head too and both hands are holding up the hem of her long dress. Linda, feeling too weak to call out, puts her hand inside the car window and beeps the horn. The person stops, and pulls back her headcover . . . 'What?'

'Who are you?' Linda calls.

'Jill.'

'Why are you running?'

'Who are you?'

'. . . Can you come over here?'

'What's your name?'

'My name's Linda. Linda.'

'Belinda?'

'No . . . Why were you running?'

'I saw this tram. It was horrible. Everyone was sitting inside like dummies. There was someone in the act of holding out her fare to the conductor who was bending over her paralysed . . . Frozen. Everyone was sittin' there as if they were bloody alive. They were all dead of course – Electrocuted . . . I could see fallen power lines on the tram. 'Orrid.'

'Where was that?' – Linda notices now that Jill has come up close that she's strikingly attractive.

'A few blocks away I think. I've never seen anythin' like that before . . . I'm a model by the way. I only came to this rotten country | 157 for a week's TV commercial modelling and they had to go and put on an earthquake. Do you know where we are? I'm lost . . . Belinda wasn't it?'

'No – Linda.' Linda feels intensely irritated, but revived. She is only tired now.

'Where were you when it happened?' she asks quietly.

'Shoppin'. Ghastly. The people. Everything down on our heads. They were like cattle. Don't worry I kicked my way out of that lot.'

'Are you English?'

'Yes. Who's this?' Jill points at Haru who is now shyly trying to clamber behind Linda's back. He bursts into tears.

'What's the matter with him?'

'His mother's probably dead.'

'. . . I expect a lot of peoples' mothers will be dead. Can he speak English?'

'Of course not. We've been speaking in Japanese.'

'That's nice. Glad I met up with you.'

'Are you?'

'Yes. But are you alright? You look like you've been playing golliwogs.'

'Thanks.'

Jill gets a hanky out of her handbag and gives it to Linda to wipe the black off her face. Jill says brightly, 'How do you expect we'll get out of all this?'

Bending down she takes in her arms Haru who is now too intrigued with Jill to struggle. And she says, as if about to briskly schedule him for a bath, supper, TV then bed, 'Just you listen to Jill. We'll get ourselves out of this fix before you can say Jack Robinson!'

Linda laughs.

'You can laugh. Just keep it up. I don't know how in hell my manager's ever going to find out where I am,' Jill says, pulling a face, 'but come on let's go.'

'Where to?'

'Anywhere'll do.'

'Better than sitting here I suppose . . .'

Jill busies with rearranging Haru and her bag in her arms. And Linda, quickly buttoning up her jacket, was flicked in the brain by the thought before she could even avoid it – And so how could it – she thought, if it only would've been me giving me something?

She slid off the car bonnet. And stood a moment, very still.
– And so how – This?

Harriet, about three o'clock in the morning, is trying to keep a handkerchief over her nose and at the same time hold the end of the bedsheet over Tatsuo's and Misa's faces. There has just passed through the house some cloud of fumes from burning plastics somewhere near. As Harriet blows her nose and dabs her streaming eyes she wonders wearily at what kind of poison has been laid in her lungs. She's almost ceased worrying about what gas or smoke will envelope the house next. Nothing can be done about it. They could all be suffocated in the next five minutes, she thinks, looking at Tatsuo and Misa.

It was not at all pleasant trying to bandage them both. Tatsuo is now stirring restlessly in sleep. Misa doesn't move, except his feverishly breathing chest. His condition has been rapidly worsening: despite the antibiotics Harriet gave him, infection from his burns and wound seems to have set in. He passed into a state of feverish unconsciousness an hour ago. There's nothing Harriet can do, without proper drugs. She's seriously doubting he will be able to survive until medical attention becomes available. And she's worried Tatsuo's feet will get infected too.

Since tucking Tatsuo and Misa in two hours ago she's been attending to flooding water pipes, rewetting the curtains, and listening to the radio – apparently, the Japan Self-Defence Forces are moving in rapidly. From overhead there has been an increasing sound of helicopters and jets. Dropping foam and water bombs, Harriet supposes. She's glad that sounds of organised activity are starting to replace the sounds of explosions and chaos.

She looks at Misa and Tatsuo again. She doesn't dare sleep. Thoughts of what could have happened to Linda keep her awake anyway. She vaguely wishes Tatsuo would wake and ask for water or something. In this cold room, lit only by the plastic torch, she is unhappy and exhausted. And lonely.

Feeling more purposeful, Linda decided that they should try to find their way back to the Chuo line, which might help them get their bearings again. Though she knew they weren't so very far away from where she lived, the blocked streets prevented them from going in that direction. But, with a bit of luck, she thought, on the way to the Chuo line they might come across a jeep or a truck full of soldiers who by now were sure to be starting to pour into the city.

The sky was now being constantly zoomed and buzzed back and forth by aircraft and helicopters, and was lit up blue and green by falling flares, the colours, however, quickly lost in the orange light of the distant fire. Activity in the streets was also becoming a bit more organised. At least in this area, which wasn't burning, people seemed to be coming out of the merely escaping-from-something stage – an in-between time now. Some people had started organising themselves into little groups for the seeking of medication and food; a few oddly uniformed individuals were shouting instructions through loudspeakers. But there was that all-pervasive look of intense mistrust and resentment on people's faces. Kicked, they were looking for something or someone to kick back. Linda, being a foreigner, and therefore conspicuous, was starting to feel a new kind of fear.

Having wet his pants, Haru is now weepily irritable. So, while inching down the street over the rubble, Linda and Jill are watching out for a pair of child's pants that just might happen to be lying about; there is plenty of other clothing scattered around.

Along this part of the shopping street, underfoot is a chopped-up carpet of mud and newspaper and ankle-deep mush. The contents of a home video and personal computer store have been pulled out into the street. A woman in a gorgeously coloured and expensive-looking kimono is standing guard with a detachable metal shelf in her hands. Regarding the girls for a moment, she calls them over, and asks them where they are going. They tell her. The woman gives them directions to her daughter-in-law's house nearby, and says they'll be safe there. Linda thanks her with much gratitude.

But turning away, Jill thinks it best to keep towards the railway line.

They are now walking past the tram full of electrocuted people Jill saw before. An old man is dragging some of the bodies off the tram but is then only leaving them in sprawled heaps. He gets back into the tram with a sprightly hop.

Linda and Jill steer clear.

The two women have become quite 'pally', as Jill put it. In other circumstances they probably would certainly have disliked each other but, as Jill gaily remarked to Linda, 'Beggars can't be choosers!'

The two of them have been taking turns at carrying Haru who, having overcome his shyness with Jill, is so pleased at having two mothers he has forgotten for the time being the absence of his real one. 'He's a one – This one, the little cheeky he is . . . Cop the way he's fiddlin' with me earlobe – The girls had better wotch out in ten years' time,' says Jill. Linda is glad of her cheer though. And Haru has found a new ear to pull and dribble into.

Linda spots at last a half burnt-out clothing shop. Giving Haru back to Jill she runs across the street and starts rummaging around in the dark shop for pants. Jill waits on the other side of the street, rocking from foot to foot with Haru on her hip.

Taking hold of a coat-hanger Linda throws it aside. Picking up another, she suddenly hears it inside her head – in that act of handing Haru over to Jill, the angel left Haru's body. Which it'd come into back at his mother's burning house. Through Haru the angel had tried to come close to her, to try to give her something, even slip her the illumination. It left, unhappy, and quite desperate, unable to do so – The shop interior going black and yellow as if she were about to faint Linda falls towards where she thinks the door is. She grabs things, pushing things aside. Outside a group of people including some uniformed men have appeared around the street corner. Seeing Linda coming out of the shop with a box the group begins jeering and flashing their torches at her. One of the men is waving a pistol. Jill yells to Linda just as the man starts firing at her. Linda ducks back across to Jill and they all begin running, the bullets pinging around their feet. 'Gawd can't they see we've got a bloomin' kid,' yells Jill, running for her life with Haru screaming in her arms.

Stopping shooting, the men are still gaining on the two women. Linda pushes at Jill to make her run faster. They come to a footbridge over a deep concrete-sided storm drain. Linda slows down a second to see how far behind the men are. Jill and Haru are halfway across the bridge when another tremor hits. The bridge collapses just as Jill and Haru make it to the other side. Linda staggers to a halt then takes to her heels again down the street along-side the stream. Panting hoarsely she keeps running and doesn't look back to see if the men are still chasing her.

A futon quilt up to her neck, Harriet is sitting with her head resting back against the wall. A little while ago she woke Misa and Tatsuo to give them the last of the antibiotics. Misa has been starting to get delirious. There's no way she could get them by herself to the small medical centre a few blocks away. But she thinks she could attempt going down there herself to join the battle probably going on there for drugs and medical attention. At this still early stage however, she doesn't think she'd be able to get any drugs – any still-functioning medical staff would probably be rationing assistance to only the most urgent cases. The only real hope is that she might soon be located by officers from the Australian embassy . . .

She is very tired, but she has gone beyond the need to sleep now. She knows she probably won't sleep until at least tomorrow, whenever that will be.

Accustomed to always planning and objectively thinking ahead, Harriet tries to mentally pick her way over the next few days. The way is unclear. From now on her life is going to be very different, she knows. The city will probably be under martial law for the next week at least, she thinks – and also, there'll be a highly likely chance that her little house could be requisitioned to provide accommodation for the homeless – at least Tatsuo would have to stay here, his apartment being wrecked . . .

She thinks of her parents in Melbourne – She hopes they haven't assumed her dead. And she muses over what's to become of her studies. The university will be closed down for weeks, at least. She thinks she could go to Kyoto to continue her studies there – Or maybe I could go up and study at the temple. The temple should be alright . . . Oh but no. It's absurd – Harriet is stricken with a moment of doubt about her whole intellectual involvement with Buddhism.

She glances over at her folder of essay notes on the table. It could almost make her wince to see how some aspects of life just insouciantly stay the same, no matter what, putting their whole faith in the future. The incredible and unknown future now. Harriet thinks of Yoshida in Hokkaido. Then she doesn't think of him, the sure-to-be-living needing no help from others to continue living. Thoughts of people like him have been blown from her mind like leaves from an autumn tree. But what about Linda? . . . Harriet thinks of the last memory she has of Linda – that of her winding her scarf around her neck as she left here with Chris . . . Now praying to the Kannon Goddess of Mercy to keep Linda safe, Harriet vows to keep and cherish her last memory of Linda, if it really is to be her last memory of her friend. Her prayer exhausting itself now, Harriet makes Linda her talisman against the uncertainty of this night. She feels guilty for the Linda of the past whom she so badly treated, and lorded it over.

Remorseful and miserable, Harriet makes up her mind it's all going to be different from now on, if and when she ever sees Linda again. She will be Linda's true friend this time; no undercutting. Linda will be moved by the examples of selfless friendship Harriet will provide. Linda, wherever she is out there in the city. Harriet thinks of the city she truly loves. Flashing, versatile, ever-changing Tokyo – It was her mirror reflection. Never has she felt so suited to a city anywhere. But what has happened to it now? She can't see it. Tokyo to her is really only what she can see of this room, a fairly undamaged room – in the torch light, little damage to be seen at all. The sensory frustration caused by her safe esconcement in this room wants to understand what has really become of the city outside. Harriet can't bear being sensorily deprived, but she doesn't dare look outside now. Sitting in a heap under her futon, she feels ugly and dull, and depressed.

The house creaks. Tatsuo rolls over in his painful sleep, muttering and whispering. Misa is lying very still, but his moving chest tells he is still breathing.

Harriet sighs. Everything seems smudged. Her sphere of living, like the black square that represents Tokyo on a map, has been dropped upon by a flick of water, run, and smudged.

She tries to recall the Tokyo of pre-nine pm last night – The trains; the suave assurance with which the trains curved into Shinjuku station; the seemingly immortal catwalk of elegant shoppers whose reflections were scattered into the sky a thousand times by the deep plate-glass windows; the peak hour traffic; the snow piling up and melting on the neon signs; Linda's clear lips and her hair tucked back over her ear as she raised her head to laugh; her own daily rising and setting over Tokyo like a source of light and life; and, above all, the way she dodged through her friends' lives; but, such recollections, such destructible images, like memos written on the torn-off corners of pages, fall, heavier than air, back to earth | 163 again, to lie in the indecipherable glamour they'd always really been in, that only her systematised energy of living gave any order to. Now, her heart wrung with grief, only ashes are what she can taste and that, from now, only that it seems. Of course it'll all be rebuilt again, the Tokyo Phoenix rising again from the ashes, the buds sprouting in herself again too, but such renewal of spirit is something which is not of now.

In her despair, Harriet feels humiliated and vulnerable. Lost, she wants to find something which will reorient herself. Full of uncharacteristic uncertainty, Harriet suddenly makes Linda the bird flying above the still burning city below. She sees Linda as alone, eyes glittering, eyes fixed on a point beyond Harriet, aiming at something through and beyond her. What Linda is aspiring to is an icon-image of goodness hung on a distant wall, a sky. No counterfeit perfection, it is resplendent and true in itself; it is seen only through itself, glimpsed beyond now slowly shutting doors, visible in all its purity only for a moment before Harriet cannot hold back the closing doors of her mind any longer. But, though she can no longer see it now, she knows it is still there, as much as the sun is always behind the clouds, to be seen again, one day.

Linda is blindly feeling her way along a wall in the dark. Her body is shuddering with cold, with sobs.

The gang gave up pursuing her, except for the man with the gun. He headed her off and drove her into an abandoned coffee shop. There, in a plush corner booth, in a litter of plaster and spilt sugar, he attempted to rape her at gun-point. For some reason he changed his mind, called her 'a skinny bitch', hit her on the kneecap with the gun handle and left, taking her panties with him.

Just as Linda was staggering out of the coffee shop, she saw a woman fighting with an adolescent over a jacket. The woman finally shoved the girl over and ran off with the jacket. The girl got up and ran after her. Trying to sit down, dizzy with weakness, Linda suddenly passed out.

When she came to, she was so suddenly and inexplicably angry she picked up the expensive-looking brooch on the ground near her. She pulled herself up and stumbled away with it. After a few steps, she threw it away. And tripped over an up-ended stereo set. The rescue-team working nearby couldn't help her – a new tremor collapsed a loose external stairwell across them.

. . . She is now feeling her way along a wall in the dark. There are no corners.

Harriet is sitting quietly under her futon, thinking of nothing in particular. She is peaceful. The smell of smoke isn't as bad as it has been. Stirring her cold stiff limbs a bit, she thinks it might be a good time now to go and try to reach the medical centre. She pushes the futon aside, and goes over to her desk. There, she writes Tatsuo a note to say where she's going, in case he wakes up. Leaving the note, and water and aspirins, on the floor by the futons, she regards Tatsuo and Misa for a moment. Tatsuo looks pale, spent. Exhausted.

Harriet crouches down to draw the blanket back over his shoulder again. Then she picks her things up, and, before leaving the room, thinks to put a stick of Lip-chap into her bag.

She lets herself out the front door and goes down the steps.

She stands at her front gate, and surveys the dark rubble-strewn street. She thinks she's going to be frightened, but she is not. Just as she is about to move off the tremor makes her grab for the old gate post on her right. In doing so she doesn't see the other sixty-year-old gate post begin to fall on top of her. She is killed, instantly.

In a narrow alley, between two burnt-out buildings Linda huddles. She thinks she might be safe here, though it's very cold. Her head is on her arm on her drawn-up knees. Her leg is slowly bleeding, and it won't seem to stop. And her left arm feels broken. The temperature is below freezing now. Weakening from exposure, Linda has never felt so empty, dirty and exhausted in her life. Without Haru and Jill now she is defenceless against herself – the spectacle of personal devastation is cruelly and inexhaustibly clear before her eyes. As clear as was the New Year Eve's snow landscape. That all might as well have been a thousand years ago. Linda cannot disassociate her own state now from the things she has seen tonight – blackened, burnt lifeless, only charred bone left. Over the chasm of the earthquake she feels her life up until last night has been rendered meaningless, futile, inconsequential – everything – Kenzo, love, the spiritual quests . . . meaningless. All the angels and enlightenment gifts they wanted to bestow now seem even more delusory than they ever were. There seems to be nothing left except the natural order which causes both earthquakes, and the cycle of the moon and tides. Nothing but that, no nourishment in that, she is huddled under that – the indifference of the night sky. As small as an atom now she could be as large as a star, but she is too tired. Everything. Nothing. Where is Haru. Where is Tatsuo or anybody. This is nobody, becoming nobody, becoming anything in the world which is cruel, ugly, beautiful or good, which is everything and nothing. She might as well be the wall she is sitting against. Might as well never be Linda again. Her very name if spoken would melt as an echo, the echo becoming an echo. Where is she. Her body is aching, her scalp itchy. She is on some little planet. The night is frigid, the night around other planets even colder. She could be there too. But truly there is nothing but thirst in her mouth and pain through her body. Forced to the limits of what the body can endure she cannot return. From the end of the plank. The cliff moves under her feet. It is a cruel thing to realise you have never really known or understood anything. Exhausted, humbled to nothing, she might now shrink smaller than an atom, so small she might almost pass through the air, and vanish forever, and die.

Tatsuo wakes up. He blinks, staring into the darkness. He is thirsty. His tongue tastes gluey and thick. Misa has rolled into the centre of the futons, and the weight of his now still body is making Tatsuo uncomfortable. Tatsuo calls out for Harriet. No one answers.

He sees the thermos of water, and the note on the floor by the futon. As he reads it he feels some alarm for Harriet, but has the relief that at least she's gone to try and get something which might relieve his pain.

Slumping his head back on the pillow he sighs softly, looks at the thermos, turns his head away, and slips back into a kind of sleep.

Where she was sitting crouched is now quite a way behind her.

Through the debris, supporting her arm, Linda is walking in as straight a line as possible, her steps strengthening as she walks – for there is nothing else left to do.

www.bookcrossing.com
BCID 796 6613397